D1384802

AMISH INN MYSTERIES™

Farmed Robbery

Marlene Chase

Annie's®
AnniesFiction.com

Library of Congress-in-Publication Data
Farmed Robbery / by Marlene Chase
p. cm.
I. Title
2017961405

AnniesFiction.com
(800) 282-6643
Amish Inn Mysteries™
Series Creator: Shari Lohner
Series Editor: Jane Haertel
Cover Illustrator: Kelley McMorris

10 11 12 13 14 | Printed in China | 9 8 7 6 5 4 3 2 1

1

Liz Eckardt settled into a vinyl seat on the bus that shuttled passengers from the airport to Pleasant Creek, Indiana. It was by far the best solution to manage the distance, saving her friends the need to drive several hours and negotiate the daunting maze of airport parking and pickup. In an hour or so she'd be back in Pleasant Creek, where Jackson Cross would meet her. She could hardly wait for his welcoming hug.

"I'll make the drive," he had said. "No need to take the bus."

But his weekday schedule was a demanding one that involved not only his thriving furniture business but his duties as mayor of Pleasant Creek. So she'd insisted on taking the bus, and he'd reluctantly agreed. They'd become friends almost as soon as she'd come to town and refurbished the Olde Mansion Inn bed-and-breakfast. Now they were dating, and Liz had never been happier.

She didn't regret walking away from her stressful job as an attorney. Boston had its advantages, but the allure of this small Midwestern town filled her even now with a settled peace and a sense of belonging. Perhaps it was only natural since it had once been her deceased mother's home, containing the Amish community she'd left behind after a deep betrayal by a devious man. For Liz, learning about her roots and kindling relationships with family members she hadn't known existed was the consummate adventure. Finding new friends who surrounded her with love and laughter only made it better.

She turned to gaze at the countryside that was quickly changing from greening fields with grazing cattle to the orderly symmetry of

Pleasant Creek. The town itself was strongly influenced by the Amish communities surrounding it. She loved the stately old library, the courthouse with its tall columns, and the pivotal point in Pleasant Creek—the clock tower, around which shops were positioned like quilt squares.

Pleasant Creek was lovely this time of year. Fruit trees blossomed, while pansies, tulips, irises, and early phlox bloomed in abundance. These were carefully tended in the town square as well as in gardens and window boxes.

But there was no more time for spring woolgathering. The bus pulled in behind the clock tower. Liz grabbed her carry-on bag and descended into the afternoon sunshine. Her larger suitcase was stowed under the bus. Once she picked that up, she'd be on her way home. *Home.* What a sweet-sounding word. The Olde Mansion Inn had become her favorite place in the world.

"Liz!" It wasn't Jackson calling her, but the voice was just as familiar.

Liz turned to smile at Sadie Schwarzentruber, the tall, white-haired co-owner of Sew Welcome, the quilting shop located inside the Olde Mansion Inn.

"Jackson had an emergency," Sadie explained, her sharp blue eyes twinkling as usual. "He asked me to meet you and drive you home." She reached for Liz's bag with deeply tanned arms still farmwife strong. In her seventies, Sadie was something of a wonder—full of zest and vitality. "It's only been a week, but we've missed you, girl," Sadie said.

"And I missed all of you." Liz returned her friend's hug. "What's the emergency?"

"Oh, nothing tragic, honey. Just an important meeting he couldn't get out of. You know him—ever the dedicated public servant. He wanted to be here, but duty called." Sadie had long been a fan of Jackson and strongly supported his relationship with Liz. Before they'd started dating, she'd said more than once, "That man better quit pussyfooting around before someone else snatches you up!"

"Come on," Sadie said. "They tell me Beans has been waiting by the door since sunup, his face glued to the glass as if he knows you're coming home today."

"I'll be glad to see him again too. You brought the van?" Liz asked as they approached the gaudy, oft-repaired three-seater van Sadie sometimes used for transporting supplies for the fabric shop.

"Sorry," Sadie said with a deep sigh. "I had to bring the Patchwork Bomb because my Jeep was stolen. Can you believe it?"

"Oh no," Liz said. Sadie loved her outrageous pink Jeep.

"My poor baby. I came out after shopping at the flea market south of town and it was gone. So far the chief has no leads, but I'm going to find the skunk who made off with her." She flung open the rear door of the van and hefted Liz's luggage inside. "You can bet your boots on that."

"I'm so sorry," Liz said when they were inside the van and Sadie's ire had settled somewhat. "But there's one good thing."

"What could possibly be good about this?" Sadie demanded.

Liz gave Sadie a sidelong smile. "The Patchwork Bomb isn't likely to be the target of a car thief."

Sadie laughed. "Actually, I'm thinking of having it painted—something ugly and nondescript. Beige maybe." She wrinkled her nose as though the thought repelled her, but then she laughed again, and they were off on the short ride to the Olde Mansion Inn.

Liz loved coming home to the elegant brick-red haven with its fresh white trim. A spring wreath of lilacs and yellow jonquils hung on the door. A colorful mat at the entrance read *Welcome*. In fact, everything about the inn said "welcome"—or at least she hoped it did—and she looked forward to seeing her friends as well as the guests who had settled here in her absence for rest and relaxation.

The door swung open even before Liz had exited the Patchwork Bomb, and Beans came lumbering toward her, pink tongue lolling over his jowls. When she had first discovered that the bulldog was a package deal with the inn, she hadn't quite known what to do. But he had become the darling of the place and had moved right into her heart.

Beans grunted with pleasure as she bent to wrap her arms around his bristly neck and accept his sloppy kisses. Not only had he roused himself from his favorite snoozing place, he was literally jumping with excitement. It was very unBeans-like. He followed Liz and Sadie inside, so close at Liz's heels that she had difficulty not stepping on him.

"You sweet old thing," Liz said. "I'll have something special for you later." In her suitcase was a long, soft toy dachshund with shaggy ears and a delightful snout perfect for chewing. She had a feeling Beans would adore his new friend.

She and Sadie negotiated the entrance and dropped Liz's bags at the door to her quarters, located off the kitchen. Liz had imagined going directly inside to wind down. She'd get out of her traveling clothes, maybe have a quick shower and even—oh, bliss!—take a nap. But Sadie was directing her through the rotunda and toward Sew Welcome, which took up two rooms on the main floor.

When she'd first taken over the inn, Liz had been surprised and not exactly delighted to learn that the quilting shop was a permanent fixture. She quickly realized, however, that the marriage of the inn and Sew Welcome was a perfectly practical one. The shop was a major attraction for the bed-and-breakfast. Its big workroom and stock of quilting and sewing supplies drew many an excited customer, some of whom became guests at the inn. Not to mention that its joint owners, Sadie Schwarzentruber and Mary Ann Berne, had become treasured friends. The rest of the Material Girls—Opal Ringenberg, Caitlyn Ross, and Naomi Mason—had also grown close to her heart. They made up a quilting group that met in the shop to sew and socialize whenever they could.

Sew Welcome was often quiet on Mondays, but when Sadie pushed open the door to usher Liz inside, several voices broke the stillness.

"Surprise!" Naomi, owner of Sweet Everything, the bakery next door to the inn, held out her arms as other friends shouted greetings.

"Welcome home!"

"You're back!"

Naomi hugged Liz, then pulled away to scrutinize her friend through chocolate-brown eyes. Closest to Liz in age, she and Liz had become fast friends.

Liz stood in the doorway, heart swelling with pleasure at seeing their faces. They were all there—except for Caitlyn, a nurse, whose hours at the hospital sometimes kept her away from gathering with the Material Girls.

"We decided an impromptu meeting was in order," Mary Ann said, her straight silver hair shining brightly. She was in her early sixties and always perfectly manicured and stylishly attired. She beamed at Liz. "Can you tell that we missed you?"

"It feels like you've been gone for a month," Opal Ringenberg said, tucking away the sweater she had been knitting. Opal, near the same age as Sadie, seemed always to be making something, often for her treasured granddaughter. "Maddy has mastered counting to five." Opal's gray hair bobbed with enthusiasm. Nothing brought her more joy than telling of Madison Ruby's accomplishments.

"You're all here just to welcome me home?" Liz asked in amazement.

"Of course," Sadie said, "but don't let it go to your head." She grinned and took command. "Let's all go to the dining room. Sarah is waiting for us. This is no ordinary meeting of the Material Girls. This is special. We're going to have a party."

They all trooped into the dining room, with Mary Ann on one side and Opal on the other, linking their arms through Liz's. The table had been set with her best china. A gorgeous bouquet of daisies and tulips bloomed in a crystal vase in the center.

Liz sat down in the place obviously designated as hers by a bright green-and-yellow balloon with the words *Welcome Home* tied to the chair. She kicked off her shoes and, shaking her head, smiled at each of them. "I've only been away for a week," she protested happily, "but I think I should go away more often if this is the welcome I get."

"Don't push it," Sadie said from where she was fanning a stack of napkins onto the tablecloth. "We actually had to meet to iron out some wrinkles in our plans for the big fund-raiser coming up, but we thought since you were coming home anyway, we'd just make a party out of it."

"So, tell us," Naomi said. "How was Maine?"

"Chilly," Liz said, reaching down to gently move Beans off her feet where he had plopped himself down. "Spring comes a bit later in that part of the country. The snow was gradually melting, but it still felt like winter to me. We didn't have much time for sightseeing anyway. The conference kept us busy with sessions all day long. But I did discover a sweet little town near Portland, right on the ocean."

"I can't imagine why you need a tutorial after running the Olde Mansion Inn all this time," Opal said, her knitting needles clicking steadily once more. "Everyone knows you're a first-class B&B hostess."

"Well, thank you. It's more to meet to exchange ideas and make sure we're all up to date on our paperwork and such. You've no idea the regulations and licensing details involved in running an inn like this. It seems like there are more and more changes and additions every year," Liz said, though she found the intricacies fascinating. She was used to keeping up with changes from her law practice and wanted the Olde Mansion Inn to be the best B&B in the area, or maybe even the state.

"Ah, here she is," Mary Ann said as Sarah Borkholder, Liz's part-time Amish employee, came in, bearing a pile of fragrant scones on a silver tray.

Sarah nodded to Liz, wisps of soft blonde hair spilling from beneath her black bonnet as she moved. A clean white apron was tied around her slender waist over her dove-gray dress.

Liz got up instinctively to take the tray. "Let me help."

"No need," Sarah said, smiling. "After all, you're the guest of honor."

"Guest? I'm no guest. And you're all spoiling me," Liz said.

At their insistence, she allowed herself to be served in the grandest style of the inn. The coffee was hot and rich, served in the china teacups usually reserved for special events. Liz savored Sarah's excellent strawberry scones and listened to her friends recount their activities during the week she'd been away.

Finally, she stood. "Since you're all here, let me get the souvenirs I brought back for you." She set her cup down and made a quick trip to the foyer to pick up her luggage. "I found some really lovely things in this adorable antiques shop that had been converted from a Colonial Revival carriage house that was built in the 1800s," she said as she returned to the dining room. "The ladies who ran it were so nice. They seemed to know exactly what I wanted for each of you, and the prices were so reasonable."

Liz had put the souvenirs in her suitcase, which was made of lightweight black polyester. It was expandable—a good thing because she'd come away with a lot more than she'd started with. She wheeled it into the sitting room and propped it near her chair. She tugged at the zipper, which instantly proved to be uncharacteristically stubborn. She'd never had trouble with it before. "I must have put more in than I thought," she said. Pulling harder, she finally made it work and flipped up the top.

Liz gasped. She stared at the items of unrecognizable clothing, then grabbed the luggage tag affixed to the side handle of the suitcase. *Reece Hoffman*. And an address in New York City.

"This isn't mine. I picked up the wrong suitcase."

Sadie leaned in to peer over her shoulder. "Who's Reece Hoffman?"

Liz stared at the name on the tag, shaking her head slowly. "She's the young woman I sat next to on the plane," she whispered, more to herself than to the others. Slowly, a picture of Reece Hoffman filling her uneasy mind, she related the story.

2

Liz was tired enough to fall asleep almost instantly once she'd boarded the flight from Portland, Maine, to Indianapolis. Miraculously, she'd been offered an upgrade to first class with its roomy seats. Now, a late boarder roused her. She looked up to see brooding brown eyes staring down at her.

"I—I'm sorry to disturb you," said a young woman with an oval-shaped face and auburn hair that fell onto narrow shoulders.

"No problem," Liz murmured groggily as the woman eased her willowy form into the aisle seat next to her.

"Looks like I just made it," the woman said as flight attendants swept down the aisle, closing the overhead baggage compartments. She stowed a small, obviously expensive bag under the seat in front of her and clicked her seat belt over her simple black dress, which somehow looked elegant on her. With a sigh, she added, "It would probably be better if I'd missed it."

Liz sat up straighter, unable to think of a response to such a statement. She glanced out the window as the plane began to move toward the runway. The B&B operators' conference had been intense, and she hadn't slept well in the hotel, waking up every few hours to unfamiliar sights and sounds. So when she finally got aboard, she'd hoped for a quiet neighbor—or the almost too-good-to-be-true possibility of a seat to herself. She took a deep breath and wondered just how much conversation she'd be required to make.

Immediately she felt chastened. It really wasn't like her to be unsociable. But she'd been surrounded by people all week and had looked forward to some downtime. Then she realized that the woman next to her hadn't spoken again after her initial remark. Perhaps she was the silent type after all. But an aura of unease seemed to permeate the atmosphere around the woman, mingling with her floral-scented perfume. She was too young to be carrying whatever burden seemed to weigh her down.

Liz turned to smile into the stunningly beautiful face. "Are you going home?"

"No. I live in New York City, but I've been in Maine on business. Now I'm making a detour to Indiana before I go back to New York." She sighed deeply as though she'd just announced some deadly portent about to materialize.

"Ah," Liz said, still feeling dull and unable to think of amusing conversation—or any conversation at all.

She noticed the young woman's slender hands in her peripheral vision. Perfectly French-manicured nails flashed like pearls as they fidgeted with the clasp on her seat belt. Liz glanced at her own hands, which were badly in need of attention. She was also painfully aware that her rumpled traveling outfit bore a small stain from the morning's on-the-run breakfast.

Next to her was a successful young woman, obviously accustomed to first class. She would likely find little in common with someone nearly two decades older—if indeed she cared to look for it. Liz felt suddenly old and dumpy, then had to laugh at herself mentally. *Old? Come on, Liz!* If Sadie, who was in her seventies, would never consider herself old, Liz certainly shouldn't.

Besides, she thought, glancing at her companion, who fidgeted as if unable to find a comfortable position, success didn't always bring happiness. A gray cloud seemed to hover over the young woman like an impending spring storm. An old quote whisked through Liz's thoughts: *What lies behind us and what lies before us are tiny matters compared to what lies within us.* Curious about what lay within her neighbor, Liz said musingly, "I'm going home to Pleasant Creek. I'll take the connector bus when we land in Indy."

Her companion mumbled something—an acknowledgment perhaps—but said no words Liz could distinguish.

"I'm Liz Eckardt," she continued. "I run a B&B in Pleasant Creek."

"Reece Hoffman," she replied.

The voice was low and well-modulated, but without any accent Liz could detect. Native New Yorkers, like Bostonians, often had a recognizable way of speaking. Reece Hoffman might have other roots.

"You're from New York, you say?"

"Yes. That is, I am now. I've been there about seven years." She raised delicately arched eyebrows. "Perfect," she said with sarcasm in her voice. "Seven's the number of perfection, isn't it?"

Liz was surprised that someone as young and cynical as Reece knew about the biblical idea that seven was the perfect number, the number of wholeness. She tucked that into a back corner of her mind and instead asked, "Do you like it in the Big Apple?"

Reece shrugged. "It grows on you," she said casually. "I started in an ad agency, but I do some modeling too." She frowned. "It keeps me busy." Then, as though bored with this attention on herself, she said, "So you run a bed-and-breakfast? I always thought that would be interesting. You know, getting to meet so many different people."

It was no surprise to Liz that this gorgeous creature was a model, but Reece was one who didn't seem terribly enthusiastic about it. Well, that was another world, one Liz knew little about. Maybe it was considered bad etiquette to be too excited about a modeling career. "You do meet interesting people," Liz agreed. "People from all over the country—sometimes the world. I used to live in Boston. I was a patent lawyer. But I found I didn't really enjoy the fast pace, the crowds, and the noise, so I decided to do something completely different. It was pretty scary at first, but now I can't imagine living anywhere else."

"Normally you wouldn't think of a move from a big city like Boston to a small town like Pleasant Creek as being scary."

Liz couldn't read the tone of the remark at all. "Well, I was still leaving behind everything and everyone I knew to start a brand-new career in another state. I could only hope for the best. I'm lucky in that I got more than the best I could have imagined."

Her real reason for settling in Pleasant Creek had been to explore the roots that connected her to her mother. She had wanted to know about the things her mother had never spoken of—why she had given up everything beloved and familiar, and had gone to a new place to begin a new life. And now, the tendrils of their lives had intermingled and were being nourished in the community Liz called home. But that seemed far too personal to share with this stranger.

The flight attendant paused in the aisle with her beverage cart. "Something for you?" she asked brightly.

Liz asked for coffee, Reece for water. *I guess when you're a model, every calorie counts.*

There was silence as they sipped their drinks. Perhaps the conversation had come to an end and Liz could resume her nap.

Dashing her hopes, Reece said, "Pleasant Creek, huh? That's not far from Reston." Idly she ran her index finger around the lip of her glass. "That's where I'm going. I used to live there."

How surprising that the small community had once been the home of this sophisticated young model. "Is that where your parents are?"

Reece stiffened, and she didn't respond for several seconds. Then, her voice suddenly cold, she said, "Sure. You could say that."

Liz turned to face Reece's rigid profile.

"They're dead."

The words fell on the air with such brash abruptness that Liz felt like she'd been slapped. "I'm sorry." Liz was unable to tear her eyes from Reece's averted face.

As quickly as she'd turned caustic seconds ago, the young woman seemed to melt, slumping in her seat. Her gaze seemed fixed on something only she could see, and her voice became softer, almost childlike. "I was sixteen. The lilacs were blooming outside my bedroom window. It was such a beautiful spring." She was silent for a long moment, and then a dreamy smile played about the perfect lips. "My parents were coming for me, to take me to the singing."

Liz drew in her breath. *The singing.* This young woman was Amish—or had been. How did a young Amish girl end up a clearly jaded, stoic model in New York City?

"Gabe was going to be there too. We would talk about the day we'd ride the wind, travel to faraway places, see what's on the other side of the country." Her face was transformed by the smile on her rose-tinted mouth, tender as a child's as she gazed into her past.

Liz was silent as her companion described an adolescent love in terms that could only be described as poetic.

"Gabe was tan and handsome, and his eyes were blue as berries in Gentian Hollow. I hoped we would marry one day. I was vain and put a sprig of lilac in my *Kapp* outside *Grossmutter's* house."

Suddenly, the words stopped. Reece put both hands up to her face, quickly covering her eyes. She took a strangled breath, as though trying to stop her tears.

Instinctively, Liz reached out to touch her hand, but Reece unbuckled her belt and flung herself out of the seat. She fled toward the back of the plane, bumping into armrests and stepping on feet that had strayed into the aisle. Liz craned her neck to watch her unsteady progress to the lavatory. She wanted to go after her but knew her presence wouldn't be welcomed. The woman had allowed herself to sink into memory and embarrassed herself in front of a virtual stranger.

Liz was curious about the contrast in the young model. She seemed to be either free of emotion or overcome by it. Liz could only hope Reece would find comfort and healing. But what had happened? What still hung over her like a pall all these years later? Liz missed her own mother, but the wound was mostly healed thanks to the friends and family she had now. What was stopping Reece from her own healing?

She tried to picture a young Reece in the simple dress and apron Amish girls wore—a dress like one Liz's own mother had worn before she was forced to leave the community. It was hard to imagine a world-weary, sophisticated New York model baking strudel, stitching a quilt, or loving a boy grown sinewy and tan from plowing fields on an Amish farm. What had happened to change her?

Liz waited, thoughts of sleep banished, book idle in her lap. And then a soft step, a slight rustle of fabric, and Reece was back, a very different Reece from the young woman who had fled down the aisle. This one was familiar—poised, fresh makeup applied, voice controlled.

"I apologize for my outburst," she said when her seat belt was once again clamped in place.

"It's all right." Liz waited, wondering how to proceed. When she was met with only silence, she ventured further, surprised at her own boldness. "My mother was Amish. She died a few years ago, but I've met many of her relatives since coming to Pleasant Creek. Most have welcomed me with open arms, though I am not Amish." She took a breath. "What happened to your parents, Reece?"

Briefly, Reece's dark, troubled eyes met Liz's inquiring ones, then focused straight ahead again with a sigh almost too soft to be heard. "There was a buggy accident. A hit-and-run with a car. *Mutter* and

Vater never had a chance. No one saw or helped, not even *Gött*." Her voice flattened with the bitterness of the words.

Liz remained silent, restraining the hand that wanted to fly to comfort the woman at her side. Reece had been a happy, expectant young girl, waiting for her parents to pick her up for the singing—a gathering typically held at the home of the family where church convened on Sunday. Liz knew it often included dinner and games, and it was an important event for youth to socialize and meet potential marriage partners. "I can't imagine how awful it was for you," she said. "I'm so sorry for your loss."

Sorry for your loss. That's what the experts said should be the only verbal response to deep grief. Yet it seemed so small in the chasm of another's pain.

"Well," Reece replied in an astonishingly level voice, "that's life, isn't it? All those pretty sentiments we're taught to believe, but in the end, you grow up and take what you can get." She held up her elegant nails and examined them.

How could she possibly be so cavalier? Did she really consider the faith she'd grown up with only a nice idea for children and perhaps the aged and senile?

"I've shocked you, I see." Reece straightened against the back of the seat and ran long fingers through her lustrous hair. "I apologize again." She gave a little shrug.

Liz swallowed. What a way to honor the memory of her parents. So why was she returning to the small town of her childhood? *It would be better if I had missed it*, she had said at the beginning of the flight. She didn't want to return at all. "I don't mean to pry," Liz began hesitantly, "but what brings you back to Indiana, to—what was the name of that town?"

Reece gave a little toss of her head. "Reston. My grandmother has been asking me to visit. Make that *nagging* me to come. Grossmutter took over my parents' farm, lately with the help of my cousin Ben. It's going well, she says." She shrugged. "Ben always had a bit of the Midas touch. And yet something . . ." The words trailed off. She pursed her lips and turned away.

Whatever the "something" was, she was not about to reveal it. A few Swiss words had slipped rather naturally from her lips, and yet it wasn't natural at all for this woman who made such effort to appear worldly. Perhaps something was hiding inside that hard shell. When Reece had related the tale, having forgotten herself so thoroughly in the telling, she had been tender, her dark eyes changing from guarded to vulnerable. Liz felt her heart expanding.

"I'll make sure Grossmutter is all right and then get back to New York," Reece added with clearly exaggerated nonchalance as she hoisted her bag onto her lap.

Flight attendants obeyed the summons to be seated as the plane began its descent into Indianapolis. Reece pulled out a compact and checked her lipstick, then examined her hair for imperfections, seemingly oblivious to Liz.

"Will someone be waiting for you at the airport?" Liz asked casually.

"Oh, no. I'll rent a car and find my own way. I prefer not to be dependent on anyone. I want to be able to leave when it suits me."

And then there was no more time for conversation, for anything more than preparing to deplane and to make her way through the maze of travelers to whatever lay beyond. The chance meeting was over, and Liz felt a strange bereavement as they taxied along the runway. "I hope you'll find everything okay with your grandmother," she said, tentatively putting a hand over Reece's slender one. "And if you need anything, or want to talk . . ." She reached into the side of her bag and pulled out a business card, then handed it to Reece. "Feel free to call me anytime."

The young woman took the card with one hand, still holding her compact in midair with the other. Suddenly the childlike longing returned to her features. "When I was little, Grossmutter used to stitch her quilts with me on her lap. I would always ask how she could work and hold me at the same time. She would give me a squeeze and say, 'You hold on to what you love.'"

The hard crust had briefly peeled back once more. Then without another word, Reece Hoffman tossed off her seat belt, stepped into the aisle, and shoved her way toward the exit.

3

Liz closed the top of the suitcase, zipped it up, and addressed her friends. "That will teach me to check the tag before running off with my luggage."

"It's an easy mistake unless you wrap a hot-pink ribbon around it or something like Sadie does," Mary Ann said. "A lot of luggage is made of this material." She bent to help Sarah clear the table of the remains of Liz's welcome home party.

"Is there a phone number on the tag?" Opal asked, tucking away her yarn and needles.

"No. Only her address in New York." Liz chewed her lip as she stared at the foreign suitcase. "But I have a phone number on mine, and I gave her my business card. I hope she'll call me." But Liz had been home at least two hours and her phone had not rung. Perhaps Reece wasn't one to unpack right away after a trip. Perhaps she'd rented her car in Indianapolis and then made a side trip or two on her way to Reston. She might have even decided to stay in a hotel near the airport tonight before making the drive.

It was growing late in the afternoon. Naomi hugged Liz a quick goodbye. "So sorry about the mix-up," she said. "It must feel weird to know someone might be rummaging through your private things right now. I hope she calls soon."

"Including the souvenirs you promised us!" Sadie said with a crooked grin.

Liz sat down, sending the balloon bobbing against her chair. She pressed her foot idly against Beans's warm body. He hadn't stirred since he settled next to her when the party began. Now he grunted and stretched himself out under the table by her feet. Sadie crossed her arms over her chest thoughtfully. "What do you want to do?" That was Sadie's way. When stuff happened, she didn't waste time fussing over it. She decided on a plan of action and went with it.

"Well, Liz said, considering her options, "I could wait for her to call me, but I want to fix this as soon as possible."

"Right. Then, let's go find her." Sadie leaned forward eagerly. "Reston, you say?"

"She said her family farm is located there. I don't know the name of her grandmother, or even if it's the same as hers—Hoffman."

Sadie's eyes narrowed in thought. "I don't get over to Reston often. There's not much there, actually. It's not a very progressive community, and it's a good forty-five minutes from here—maybe more depending on the time of day. Why don't we just head over? I'm sure someone in town can direct us to a farm owned by someone named Hoffman. It's a start, and maybe the lady will call while we're on the way."

"Are you sure you can spare the time?"

"I wouldn't have suggested it if I wasn't."

"It's all right," Mary Ann said. "I'll close up the shop."

Sadie jumped up and grabbed her purse. "You drive. On the way, I'll keep my eyes open for my Jeep. Somebody's got her, and I aim to find her. That bright-pink chassis won't be easy to hide."

Liz patted Beans's lumpy head in farewell with a promise to bring back his surprise, and they set out in Liz's Acura in the waning afternoon.

Liz breathed in the fresh, chilly air. It felt good to be in control of her own vehicle after depending on planes and buses. Trees held greening branches to a darkening spring sky. Flowering specimens had dropped their abundance, blossoms giving way to leaves. Lawns, brown and dry through the long winter, glowed with new greenery. As they drove deeper into the countryside, plowed and planted fields seemed to tremble with vitality.

"I never get tired of these old sights," Sadie said. "Lived here all my life, and every spring still makes me want to dance." She gave Liz, who was snickering, a sidelong glance. "What? You know I love to dance. I may not be a spring chicken, but spring still sets my toes tapping!"

"Spring's my favorite time too."

Sadie suddenly pounded her fist on the dashboard. "I miss my Jeep! I drive her around every spring just looking at the new plants and flowers and such. It helps me get into the season. I left her alone for just a few minutes. I dumped the items I bought at the flea market—a painting that reminded me of one my grandmother had and some costume jewelry pins, nothing that would have value to anyone else—into the back, locked it, and went across the street to the fruit stand. When I came back, my car was gone. I paid next to nothing for the items, so I'm not too upset about them, but my Jeep!"

Liz glanced sidelong at her friend's scowl.

"I'm going to take a peek in Simon Payne's garage," Sadie continued. "That kid's always kicking up mischief somewhere. Usually he's tearing around on his motorcycle, scaring cats and chickens. Maybe he's graduated to stealing cars from innocent folks. I don't trust him any farther than I can spit. Which is admittedly pretty far. But you know what I mean."

"Jackson and I paid a visit to Simon the winter Naomi and I got run off the road. I really don't see him as a car thief." Liz felt herself smiling at the memory. "Surely the chief will get a lead on your Jeep soon." She changed the subject, distracting Sadie with conversation about the coming town market event, which Sadie and Mary Ann had been working toward for several months, sponsoring quilters and crafters from Sew Welcome. It seemed to get Sadie's mind off her loss, at least for a while, though Liz wondered why anyone would steal a pink Jeep of indeterminate age. The thing wasn't exactly inconspicuous. Whatever the reason, heaven help the thief when Sadie caught him—or her.

A slightly crooked sign announced the town of Reston: *Come on in and 'Rest on' us. Population 3,200.* "Is that corny or what?" Sadie exclaimed as Liz groaned at the sign. "I love it!"

Liz pulled into a gas station with pumps that resembled museum pieces. "Let's try here. Looks like this station has been around awhile."

A middle-aged man in a white T-shirt stretched to the max over his burgeoning stomach emerged from a bay where he had been working on a rusty pickup truck. He greeted them with a greasy tire wrench in his beefy fist.

"Does that mustache remind you of anything?" Sadie asked as they neared the garage.

Liz shook her head.

"An attachment for a vacuum cleaner."

Liz grinned. Life with Sadie was never dull. "Don't tell him that. I think he'd be less inclined to help us after that."

"Hoffman place is a good six miles out on Tate Road," the attendant said in response to their question. "Ain't much else out that way. I expect you'll find it easy enough." He took off his cap to scratch his balding head. "You ladies want gas?" When Liz declined, he plopped his dirty cap on his head again and turned back to the truck.

Sadie called to his retreating bulk, "You seen anything of a pink Jeep around here?"

"Nope." He rolled his eyes, gave his head a shake, and peered back under the truck's hood.

After reaching Tate Road, Liz checked the odometer so she'd know when they'd traveled the six miles the gas station attendant had estimated. They passed farms of various sizes, grassy pastures of grazing cattle, and fields just beginning to reveal carefully planted rows of what was probably wheat or corn or soybeans. Then the road seemed to contract as an overgrowth of greenery converged on it. They pushed ahead on the dusty gravel road.

"Pretty remote out here," Sadie said. "They could do with some road repair. But I suspect the natives are used to it." She pointed to a partially hidden sign, indicating a one-way junction to the right. "That might be the entry to the Hoffman place, but they certainly aren't big on advertising."

Liz turned and followed a snaky road bounded on both sides by vegetation, then pulled into a clearing where the farm became visible. It appeared well-tended, its plain buildings and sheds in good repair—an ordinary Amish farm—except, perhaps, for the iron gate, which was fortunately open.

Once inside the property she circled around to the house—a two-story white clapboard with lilac bushes in full bloom surrounding it. Gardens and fields showed no sign of workers, but the day was largely spent, with little sunlight remaining. She hoped they wouldn't be interrupting the family's supper hour. No buggy was in evidence, but a late-model car shimmered under a row of sycamore trees—Reece's rental perhaps. Two other cars were partly visible behind a metal garage-like structure.

"You say this farm belongs to the young woman's grandmother?" No doubt Sadie wondered, as Liz did, about the modern vehicles on an Amish farm. "What was that name again?"

"Reece Hoffman," Liz replied. "She says her parents were killed in a buggy accident when she was sixteen, leaving the grandmother to run the farm." Odd that there was no buggy in sight, but perhaps it was stowed away in the barn.

"Reece Hoffman," Sadie murmured thoughtfully. "I don't remember her, but I do remember a couple from Reston being involved in a tragic road accident a number of years ago." She released a sigh. "Still happens, you know. More often than people think."

"That's terrible. I've seen drivers get extremely close to buggies. It terrifies the horses." Liz shook her head. "Such a shame—a couple killed and leaving a child behind. I can understand Reece's bitterness." She parked, and she and Sadie climbed out. "But she's young to be so hard. At least she's come to visit her grandmother, who has been wanting to see her. Maybe she cares more about her family than she lets on."

They walked to the door, still hearing no sounds and seeing no one, not even a family dog. The silence sent a little shiver down Liz's spine. She'd be glad to get her suitcase and return to Pleasant Creek. Before she could knock, a door opened, as though they were expected. Had someone been watching and seen them approach?

A clean-shaven man dressed in a short-sleeved polo shirt and khaki pants smiled politely at them. Good looks apparently ran in the Hoffman genes, though sandy hair was a disconcerting match for his dark eyes and tanned skin. His husky frame filled the doorway, but he made no move to step back as he glanced from Sadie to Liz. "Good afternoon, ladies." There was a question in his mellow voice, but his eyes radiated confidence and shifted briefly to a suitcase just inside the door. A suitcase that looked like hers.

Liz had expected black pants, suspenders, and a beard, but this man was dressed in the English manner. "I'm Liz Eckardt from Pleasant Creek," she began. "And this is Sadie Schwarzentruber. We're looking for Reece Hoffman—"

"So you're the one who took my cousin's suitcase," he said, interrupting Liz's introduction and examining her closely. He was sizing her up, and a small smile emerged. "I have your suitcase right here, Ms. Eckardt." He reached down to pick it up with well-muscled arms. He nodded to the suitcase still in Liz's grasp. "I'll be glad to take that off your hands. A shame you had to drive clear over here. I'm Benedikt Hoffman. Most people call me Ben. I'm Reece's cousin. But I'm afraid she isn't feeling well and is lying down. She said she would call you when she woke up."

Puzzled, Liz stared into the handsome face. "Oh, I'm sorry. Is she—?"

"Just a headache," he interrupted again. "Long journey and all that. I'm sure she'll be fine. She—uh—wasn't aware of the mix-up right away, but I'm certain she would want me to thank you and apologize for causing you any trouble."

"Oh, it wasn't any trouble," Liz said, glancing around the man to peer inside. A small foyer led to a staircase. Drawing her gaze back to Ben, her eye caught a swish of dark-blue skirt and graying hair off to his right. *The grandmother, perhaps on her way to prepare a cup of tea for her ailing granddaughter?*

"Well, once again, our thanks," Ben said, stepping back and reaching for the door.

Liz and Sadie stepped back as the door closed quickly.

"Did you get the feeling that Mr. Benedikt Hoffman was giving us the bum's rush?" Sadie asked under her breath as they retraced their steps to the car and got inside.

Liz shrugged. "Oh, I don't think so. He was polite enough. I'm sure he's busy."

"He's too smooth by half," Sadie said, a little grumpily. "He has a pretty face, but handsome is as handsome does, I always say."

"You're just ticked off about your Jeep," Liz said, laughing. "I'm sorry. I'd be upset too if someone had snitched my wheels. Besides, if you don't trust a handsome face, what about Jackson?"

"Jackson's proved himself. Did that woman—Reece—seem ill when you left her?" Sadie pushed out her lips again in a kind of tacit disapproval.

"She seemed okay—but maybe she gets migraines or something. Who knows? At least I got my suitcase back."

"Well, you'd better check it carefully—make sure nothing's missing."

"Sadie, you do have a suspicious mind."

"No, I have a practical one."

Silently, Liz recalled the shattered look in Reece's eyes when she had told her about her parents' death, how deeply disturbed she had been. "Well I'm sure her grandmother is taking good care of her. I'm sorry we didn't get to meet the grandmother, but from what we could see of her, she seemed to be busy in the kitchen."

Sadie didn't respond until Liz had maneuvered the winding driveway to the road. "I saw someone in there too, but that was no Amish woman," she declared.

Liz turned in surprise. "What makes you say that?"

"Her shoes. No laces and cut low in the front like a slipper."

"You've got sharp eyes. But I guess it's none of our business what the Hoffmans choose to wear—or do, for that matter." She paused, feeling unaccountably sad. "I did hope to see Reece—just to make sure she's all right. She's been dealt a rough hand in life. I really wanted to help her somehow." The sad, dark eyes and her own sense of failure weighed heavily on her heart the whole drive home.

4

Liz woke early the next morning, luxuriating in the pleasure of her own bed. She had slept like a rock and felt more rested than she had in days. She pushed back the covers and swung her feet to the floor.

When she and Sadie had returned to Pleasant Creek from the Hoffman farm, Liz had gone straight to bed after inspecting her suitcase. Everything was as she had left it, including the souvenirs she had purchased for her friends. She smiled as she dressed, anxious to get into the kitchen and prepare breakfast for guests of the inn, some of whom she had yet to meet in person.

Sarah arrived within minutes of Liz's switching on the lights in the kitchen, and they set about preparing muffins, bacon, a scrambled-egg casserole, and fruit. A bed-and-breakfast was doomed if the first meal the guests consumed wasn't hot, fresh, and delicious. "It's good to have you back," Sarah said softly, hanging her coat on a peg in the small closet off the kitchen. Her large green eyes glowed with the serenity that always seemed to radiate from her.

She'd been eighteen when she first came to work with Liz at the Olde Mansion Inn. Since then, she'd married Isaac Borkholder, the son of Liz's cousin Miriam, and proved herself indispensable time and again. Liz smiled as she spooned fruit into small glass bowls. She was part of the family now—a family she had not known existed before coming to Pleasant Creek and discovering her roots.

"You can't imagine how glad I am to be back," Liz told the young woman, who was tying an apron over her plain blue dress. "The conference was helpful, and I met some interesting people." She couldn't help thinking about Reece with a pang of regret. "But right here at the inn is the best place to be," she finished. "I'm anxious to meet our guests. Tell me, how are the Holmes sisters?"

Vera and Violet Holmes were twins, returning for yet another visit to the inn. Retired teachers, they were enamored with all things quilting and loved being right on the premises with the Sew Welcome Shop. "They are much the same, only Violet is rounder and Vera is . . ."

Sarah hesitated, never one to ascribe a negative aspect to anyone, even the somewhat cantankerous Vera, who dominated her more passive sister and could at times try one's patience. "Vera is still Vera," she pronounced with a knowing smile. "They're in the Rose of Sharon Room, of course," she added. "They are quite happy about that."

The Rose of Sharon was their favorite room, with its white vintage furniture and Gene Stratton-Porter prints of birds.

"And the lady from New Jersey—Ms. Penelope Stryker, isn't it? Has she checked in?" Liz recalled the lady had said she was a business attaché, whatever that was.

"She checked into the Sunset Room yesterday afternoon. But she went out shortly afterward. I didn't see much of her." Sarah frowned and absently adjusted the glass she had just set in its place. "It was odd, though. She was all fancied up. She's quite beautiful really, but I was sure I saw a bruise around her left eye—despite the heavy makeup she was wearing."

"Hmm. What was she like?"

"She's all right, just a bit demanding." Ever the careful chooser of words, Sarah was probably erring on the side of grace in her description of Ms. Stryker.

Penelope. An old-fashioned name. Perhaps she went by a nickname. When the retired couple from Chicago arrived tomorrow, the current guest list would be complete. There was something so satisfying about the kind of hospitality she could offer at the Olde Mansion Inn. It was a way of sharing her heart and passing on the kindness and hospitality she herself had received from others.

"Did you get your suitcase back?" Sarah asked as she filled the coffee urn.

"Yes, and I returned the one I picked up by mistake. That's something I won't let happen again. Next time I travel I'm going to attach the brightest piece of fabric I can find to it. There'll be no mistaking it then, and I doubt anyone will accidentally walk off with it." She placed a pan of muffins into the oven. "I didn't get to see my friend from the plane, though," she added. "The man who met us at the door said she wasn't feeling well. My suitcase was right by the door and he just handed it over, and that was that." Liz briefly described what she had learned about Reece's background during the flight. "I wish I could have helped her."

Sarah gave her quiet smile. "I'm sure just having someone listen with kindness did help her, in however small a way. You don't give yourself enough credit, Liz."

Liz and Sarah finished preparing breakfast and setting everything out in warming pans on the sideboard in the dining room. The aroma of fresh blueberry muffins filled the room, where Sarah had set the table with pastel paisley napkins and a vase of purple irises in the center, making the whole room seem bright and fresh. Soon other flowers would be popping their heads up outside, destined to adorn the dressers and tables of the Olde Mansion Inn. Slow steps on the staircase heralded the first guest to come down for breakfast.

"Well, here you are now," Vera Holmes said, emphasizing *now* and causing the lines around her pursed lips to deepen. She squinted over gold-rimmed spectacles. She wore a tweed jacket over a long brown skirt, putting Liz in mind of a British dowager. "I rather expected you to be on hand when we checked in yesterday," Vera said sharply. "In any case, you're here now, and everything seems quite satisfactory."

Liz felt herself smiling. If Vera ever cracked a smile, she might actually crack. Still, there was something engaging about the woman, whose adherence to strict moral standards and proper etiquette was legendary. Liz was fond of her in spite of her apparent sharpness. "I'm so glad to see you again, Miss Holmes."

"It's quite all right to call me 'Vera,'" the woman corrected her, a glint of humor appearing in the dark eyes. "I believe we are familiar enough for that." She turned as Violet entered the dining room.

"Sister, isn't it wonderful to see Miss Eckardt again?" It was a mild response to her sister's sharp tone. The gentle Violet deferred to her sister in most matters but often had to pour oil on troubled waters. Wearing her signature purple, she floated into the dining room, a fuller, softer version of her sister. She grasped Liz's outstretched hand and pulled her into a hug. "We couldn't wait to come again," she gushed, the pink blush on her cheeks deepening.

"I'm so glad you're here, Violet. I'm sorry I wasn't on hand to greet you when you arrived."

She began to explain her absence due to the conference, but Violet interrupted. "Don't worry. Sarah took care of everything—and we absolutely love our room, as usual." She smiled. "You're so good to reserve that room for us. And you didn't forget the purple violets. Bless you, dear!"

"Come along!" Vera ordered. "Our breakfast will be getting cold." She proceeded to help herself at the serving table.

Violet followed, exclaiming about the "delectable feast" before them. *Of which she will heartily partake*, Liz thought, recalling Violet's healthy appetite. It was nice to have her hard work appreciated.

Violet looked around and, seeing Sarah, gave her a warm smile.

Then she suddenly frowned. "I don't see Miss Stryker. I had hoped to make her closer acquaintance this morning."

There was a loud sniff from Vera. "I don't doubt she'll be too tired to get up after staying out until all hours of the night. 'Early to bed, early to rise' is still the proper way to conduct oneself."

"I heard nothing once my head hit the pillow," Violet said happily, taking two large scones from the bread basket.

Ms. Stryker had been assigned the Sunset Room with its blend of contemporary and antique furnishings, accented with carefully chosen and brightly colored wall art and cushions. Liz hoped its occupant wouldn't make late hours a habit. Sarah had said she'd gone out shortly after checking in. Well, sleeping in was what vacations were all about. And guests were free to come and go.

Breakfast passed pleasantly with the back-and-forth banter of Violet and Vera. When it came time to wash up and tend to the housekeeping of the inn, Penelope Stryker still had not appeared. Liz set aside a plate of muffins and fruit just in case.

———

Liz, Naomi, and Sadie had planned a quick trip to the town hall to see about the permit that was needed for the Material Girls to participate in the impending town market event. Naomi met up with Liz and Sadie after leaving her assistant, Candice, to handle things at the bakery. They walked the short distance to the town hall.

"I wonder why it's taking so long to receive our permit," Naomi said. "We requested it several weeks ago."

"I understand the city is hiring a temporary consultant to organize events for the town and coordinate the advertising," Liz said. "That may have slowed things down a bit."

"Since when do we need a permit?" Sadie wanted to know. "I don't see that anything has been wrong with our organization before." Liz tucked her arm through Sadie's. "I'm sure it was just an oversight." Liz smiled as she spied Jackson at the end of the hall.

He was walking toward them, handsome in a royal-blue button-up shirt and gray slacks. His tall physique and strong bearing made him a perfect fit for the town hall. *Or anywhere*, Liz thought, admiring his strong jaw and the mass of brown hair, only slightly mussed—probably from running a hand through it in the process of thought. She'd pointed it out once, and he'd been totally unaware of the habit.

"Liz," Jackson called, coming to a stop beside them. "Now I see for myself that you're home safely." He gave Liz a quick hug, then turned to Sadie. "Thanks for filling in for me." He extended a hand to greet Naomi, then returned his gaze to Liz with a raised eyebrow. "I'm glad to see you all, but what brings you to my neck of the woods?"

"We're here to see what happened to our permit to participate in the town market event," Liz said, enjoying the warmth in Jackson's face. Maybe absence really did make the heart grow fonder.

"It's been weeks since we sent in our application," Naomi put in, "and we're getting concerned."

"Is there some reason for this unwarranted delay?" Sadie asked testily, narrowing her eyes at him.

Liz gave Sadie a tiny nudge with her elbow. Sadie was in a pugnacious mood this morning. No doubt her stolen Jeep had something to do with it. She glanced up at Jackson, whose curiosity had given way to confusion and concern.

"There have been some computer malfunctions here lately, but I'm sure there's no problem with your application." His eyebrows knit suddenly, then relaxed. "Actually, a temporary consultant has been brought on to assist with community event scheduling. Let me introduce you. We'll get this cleared up."

"Naomi and I will wait here," Sadie spoke up suddenly. "No need for us all to go barging in like a band of thieves. Besides, I've been meaning to have a look at that lobby display of old Pleasant Creek maps."

But Liz knew what her friend was up to. Testy mood aside, Sadie was engaging in her usual matchmaking antics to give her and Jackson some time alone. She grinned and headed down the long hallway with him.

"How was your trip?" Jackson asked when they had moved out of earshot.

"It was really—"

"Actually," he interrupted, humor in his voice, "don't tell me now. Say you'll have dinner with me tonight. I want to give you my undivided attention when you give your report."

She laughed and gave him a quick glance, trying to hide her eagerness to accept. "I think I could fit you into my schedule. What time?"

"How's six thirty? No, better make it seven. There's a board meeting that sometimes goes over."

"Seven's good."

They turned down another hallway. Jackson stopped abruptly at the first office, knocked, and opened the door at the "Come in" from the other side.

An attractive woman sat at a desk, upon which perched a shiny new placard with the name *Penelope Stryker*. Huge azure eyes ringed by long, black, obviously false lashes met Liz's. Framing her tanned, heart-shaped face was platinum hair cut long enough to curve along her jaw in the front and short in the back. Her glossy pink lips stretched in a polite smile.

"Penny, I'd like you to meet one of Pleasant Creek's finest citizens—Liz Eckardt," Jackson said. "Liz, this is Penelope Stryker, the consultant I was telling you about."

"Liz Eckardt?" Her voice carried an exaggerated cosmopolitan drawl. "The woman who owns the delightful B&B where I'm staying?" Penelope Stryker leaned back and planted both jeweled hands on the arms of her desk chair. The bright pink silk of her blouse shimmered, perfectly matching her lipstick. A white jacket was draped over the back of the chair, and on a credenza behind her lay a wide white hat with an enormous pink feather blooming from a black ribbon band.

Liz thought she might have responded but wasn't sure in the presence of the consultant's over-the-top extravagance and a painful awareness of her own plain persona. She searched for evidence of a bruise on the woman's face, but her complexion was perfect—disgustingly perfect. Either she was a quick healer, or what Sarah had seen was a smudge from heavy mascara.

"I was just telling His Honor at our meeting yesterday about your charming establishment," Penny continued, fluttering her eyelashes at Jackson. "I've stayed at a lot of B&Bs around the country, and the Olde Mansion Inn is . . . well . . ." But she seemed too consumed with her own melodrama to complete her rave. She stood, revealing a figure most women would die for, and extended a hand. "I'm pleased to meet you at last," she said. "Your sweet little helper was good enough to check me in quickly, as I had a great many things to attend to at the office."

His Honor? Sweet little helper? With herculean effort, Liz found her voice. "Nice to meet you, Ms. Stryker," she managed. It came out a little choked in spite of her best efforts.

"Please. Call me Penny. I look forward to making friends of Pleasant Creek's new citizens, now that I've returned after so many years. Actually, I have an aunt not far from here. Perhaps I can be helpful to her. She's growing a bit forgetful these days." She made an exaggerated gesture with a well-toned arm. "As Jackson can tell you, I went to high school in this fair town. When this temporary consulting job became available, I knew I just had to return." She giggled, batting her baby blues at Jackson once more. "Kind of like a penny, but not a bad one, I hope. What can I do for you today?"

Liz exchanged a quick glance with Jackson. Had they gone to high school together? There was only one in Pleasant Creek, after all. And they certainly seemed to be acquainted. She'd said they'd had a meeting the day before. Was Penny the "emergency" that had kept him from coming to pick her up at the bus depot? She drew a breath. "My friends and I are members of a club that exhibits quilts and other crafts. We have been waiting to receive a permit for the market event. We sent in an application some time ago, but we haven't heard anything. Do I understand that you are handling these matters?"

"Ah, yes, the town market. Such a delightful idea," Penny said. Then, clearing her throat, she took on a more official persona. "I haven't had time to thoroughly review all the applications on my desk." She pointed to a pile of folders near her nameplate. "The town wants to make the market a truly memorable and successful event. We must get everything just right. But I'm sure you'll be hearing from us very soon." The pink lips stretched into a patronizing smile.

Jackson squared his shoulders and said, "I can personally vouch for Liz's group. Please handle her application today and give her a confirmation call."

"Of course," she said quickly. Her cheeks reddened. "And since I'm staying at the Olde Mansion Inn, I'll confirm it in person."

Can't wait, Liz thought dryly. "Thanks," she said, her tone as polite and professional as she could make it. She took a step toward the door. "Oh, and welcome to the Olde Mansion Inn. I hope you'll enjoy your stay." But Liz had a sinking feeling that she herself might not.

5

When chores were finished and she'd taken Beans out after he ate, Liz dressed for her dinner date with Jackson. "What do you think?" she asked the jowly bulldog. "The blue-and-white print dress?" She did a slow turn in front of the mirror and awaited his appraisal.

Beans made no move as he eyed her lazily from his bed.

"That good, huh?" She frowned and held up a jade shift. "How about this one with a belt?"

Beans emitted a grunt of approval—or, more likely, a precursor to a snore—and closed his eyes.

"Your enthusiastic opinion is noted," she said fondly. "The blue-and-white it is." She added a teardrop pendant of blue crystal and surveyed herself in the mirror with a critical eye. The dress had served her well for several springs, and she felt comfortable in it. *Passable*, she thought, but in her mind's eye she saw an hourglass figure in satiny pink, platinum hair framing a stunning face, and eyes like blue Delft saucers.

She sighed and turned away from the mirror. *Don't do that*, she told herself sternly. Comparisons could be deadly.

"We went to high school together," Penny had said earlier that day. Liz tried to shake the image of the woman who had taken a job in Pleasant Creek and was also a guest at the inn. Their paths would be certain to cross frequently, and Penny was obviously making a play for Jackson. Why couldn't she just stay with her aunt instead of at the inn? She smoothed her dress. "He'll like me as I am or not," she whispered fiercely to the mirror and, grabbing a small box from her dresser, she left Beans to his doggy dreams.

Jackson rang the front doorbell at five minutes before seven. He appeared only slightly harried and had found time to change into an Oxford shirt the color of a summer sky. He was smoothing the lapels of a gray sport coat when she opened the door. "Not late, am I?"

She stepped back to usher him in. "Five minutes early, actually," she said, warming to his light kiss.

Liz was glad he had time for a date. Spring was a busy season for the town, and Jackson took his civic responsibilities seriously. He was also committed to his furniture business. It wasn't unusual for him to work late there when the need arose. Very little grass grew under his feet.

He smiled at her. "I've been looking forward to this all day."

"Let me grab a jacket and turn on the porch lights," she said.

"Sure thing." He stooped to pet Beans, who had apparently heaved himself up at the sound of the doorbell and followed her into the foyer. "Bet you're glad to have your friend back, aren't you, boy?"

Beans grunted happily and retreated to his favorite place on the rug near the front door.

Liz took the arm Jackson offered her. It felt good having her arm linked in his. Surely he felt it too, and she had nothing to worry about from a flirtatious temporary consultant, even if she did work with him every day.

They had just reached the curb when a white BMW screeched to a halt beside Jackson's dark sedan. The passenger door opened, and a vision of pink and white burst out, as if Liz had summoned her with a thought.

It was only natural that Penelope should return to the inn after a day of consulting or whatever it was she was doing here in Pleasant Creek. But she seemed to have timed her arrival to coincide with Jackson's. Liz took a deep breath. Their paths were crossing sooner than she'd expected or hoped.

Penny's huge eyes widened as she glanced from one to the other. Clearly she had noticed Liz's hand on Jackson's arm, signaling the warm camaraderie between the two. She was speechless at first, but recovered herself. "Well, here you are, Liz," she simpered. "How nice to see you—both." She raised a perfectly shaped eyebrow as if she'd caught them doing something wrong.

Liz was aware of Jackson nodding a greeting. Steeling herself, she said, "Good evening. I trust you'll find everything satisfactory. The Holmes sisters can help you if you need anything while I'm out. They're frequent guests here at the Olde Mansion Inn."

"How nice," Penny said, flashing a smile that didn't quite reach her eyes. She pulled a small envelope from her fashionable purse. "I have your permit—as promised," she said regally and, favoring Jackson with another sweep of her long, black eyelashes, placed the envelope in Liz's hand. "Well, have a nice evening," she finished and sauntered toward the door, four-inch heels wobbling a bit unsteadily on the cobbled walk.

"You too, Penny," Jackson called out. He helped Liz into his car, closed the door, and got in behind the wheel. Liz waited for some comment about the new consultant, but he said only, "You up for Pasta Heaven tonight?"

It had become one of their favorite places, with offerings like Divine Bruschetta, Cherubic Tortano, and Blissful Lasagna. They were corny names for traditional Italian entrées, but that was part of the charm.

"I could go for some Eternal Breadsticks," she said and cracked her window open. It was unseasonably warm for a spring evening and Liz enjoyed the fresh breeze on her cheeks as they made the short drive.

Dinner was delicious as usual as Liz told Jackson all about the conference. He listened attentively, asking question after question. While they were launching into the final course, Angelic Tiramisu,

Liz reached into her purse and pulled out the little box she'd grabbed from her dresser. "I picked this up in Maine," she said. "I thought you'd like it." She felt suddenly shy as she held out the box.

He accepted it and opened it to reveal a compass paperweight encircled in a forged-brass ring. The perfect accompaniment for desk or office, it was made of fine lacquered brass and had been advertised not to tarnish or show fingerprints.

She watched him cradle the paperweight in his strong hands, which showed the ruggedness of a working man. "This is fantastic, Liz. Thank you." His voice was low and quiet. He grasped her hand across the table. "Maybe I'll keep it in my pocket so I don't lose my way," he said, a smile lighting his face.

"Just a little something I thought you'd like," she said. "You almost didn't get it, though. Seems someone else has a suitcase just like mine, and we got them mixed up at the airport. I got a big surprise when I opened my luggage and didn't recognize a thing inside it."

"Those things happen. I'm glad you got them switched back."

"Me too. All's well that ends well."

But had it ended well? Reece's sad eyes still bothered Liz. Their meeting on the plane had seemed destined somehow, for she had felt the burden of the young woman's pain and desperately wanted to help her. She thought it had also meant something to Reece, who had stared with longing at the business card she had given her, then tucked it quickly away. But Reece hadn't even phoned to thank Liz for driving clear to Reston and searching out her grandmother's farm.

"Good thing there were addresses on those suitcases." Jackson signaled the waiter for more coffee.

"Well, the lady who got my luggage had a New York address on hers. She was going to visit family in Indiana—Reston, actually. We were seated together on the plane." She paused, thinking about how Reece had bolted up the aisle in a rush of tears. "I expected her to contact me," Liz continued. "She had the address on my suitcase and a business card I gave her."

Jackson raised an eyebrow. "But she didn't call?"

Liz shook her head. "When I didn't hear from her after several hours went by, Sadie and I searched her out. It wasn't easy. I knew her name and that she was visiting family who live on a farm in Reston. Her name is Reece Hoffman, but I had no idea if the family name was also Hoffman or where the farm was."

"Knowing you, it probably wasn't that hard to track down," he said meaningfully.

She shrugged. "We asked around. The attendant at a gas station in town knew a Hoffman family and told us how to find the farm."

"I'm sure your new friend was grateful that you went to all that trouble," Jackson said.

"That's just it—I still haven't heard anything from her. We didn't even see her when we were there at the farm. The man who answered the door said Reece wasn't feeling well. He had my suitcase right by the door and seemed very anxious for Sadie and me to leave." Liz paused, absently tracing the rim of her cup. She shivered involuntarily, though it was warm enough in the restaurant that she had removed her sweater. "The whole thing was strange."

"Maybe when she's feeling better, she'll contact you," Jackson offered.

"I hope so. Anyway, I've heard my suitcase isn't the only thing to go missing in Pleasant Creek recently, nor is it the worst. Sadie's really upset about her stolen Jeep."

"I bet she is," Jackson said. "She's been down at the police station every day since it happened, and I think she's checked out every garage in Pleasant Creek, but there's still no word on the perpetrator."

Liz pushed her coffee cup away, declining any further refills. "How in the world does someone hide a pink Jeep?"

"And why steal it in the first place? Don't let Sadie know I said this, but really there's nothing special about it—well, aside from its shocking color." He drummed his fingers quietly on the table, his brow furrowed. "Did she say where she was when it was taken?"

"The flea market. You know how she is about searching for unexpected treasures. And to give her credit, in the past she's found some items worthy of an antiques reality show." Liz smiled. "She once found a first-edition *Walden* by Thoreau that she only paid a dollar for. She told me they go for hundreds online, sometimes thousands."

"Did she mention finding anything particular this time?"

"She said something about a painting that reminded her of her grandmother and a handful of assorted costume jewelry pins. She said she paid a pittance for everything. Besides, if someone was after her flea market finds, why not take them and leave the Jeep?"

"Just what I was wondering." Jackson spooned up the last bit of his tiramisu.

"She said she stowed the things in the back of the Jeep and then went across the street to the fruit stand. When she came back a short time later, the Jeep was gone. She thinks somebody like that Simon Payne ripped it off just for meanness or for a joyride."

Jackson grinned. "Simon's still stirring up mischief, I hear. I'm sure Chief Houghton won't leave that stone unturned. But I'm a little worried about what will happen when Sadie catches up with him, if he did it."

Liz laughed. "Remember when we snuck into his garage looking for a motorcycle?"

"Yes. You roped me into snooping, as I recall. You have a penchant for mystery that keeps getting us into trouble." He gave her an admiring grin that said he didn't mind. "But it's getting late. I suppose we'd better go, or they'll be chasing us out."

They drove back under a clear sky with a smiling crescent moon and a smattering of stars. They didn't talk much. It was a hallmark of their relationship that they could be silent together and still feel connected. Jackson parked at the inn, and then they decided to take a short stroll around the grounds of the inn, neither quite ready for the evening to end.

"Someone's making use of your gazebo," Jackson said as they passed from a distance. He nodded in the direction of the octagonal white structure, complete with climbing vines and bordering rhododendrons.

Inside was an elderly couple, the woman in a lavender skirt that flowed to chubby ankles. "That's Violet Holmes," Liz said. "She and her sister, Vera, are guests again this year." She peered at the figure of a white-haired gentleman talking closely to Violet. "And that, if I'm not mistaken," she added brightly, "is Stefan Meyer, my handyman."

"I think you're right," Jackson said. "Well, I'm happy for them." He waved as they passed, but neither Violet nor Stefan looked up, so engrossed were they in each other's company.

"You never get too old," Liz said quietly, warming to the vision. Jackson gave her hand a squeeze and they continued their walk. It was nearly dark when they finally returned to the front of the inn. Jackson gave her a hug and a sweet kiss, then strode off down the sidewalk, giving her a smile and a wave as he climbed into his car.

She waved back. What a lovely evening it had turned out to be. And yet now that she was alone, she couldn't get Reece Hoffman out of her mind.

6

A loud sneeze erupted, signaling the arrival of the first guests to enter the dining room for breakfast. Liz looked up from the table where she had just set a platter of steaming Amish-made sausages to see Violet holding a flowery purple handkerchief to her nose.

"Well, it's no wonder you've got the sniffles after sitting out there in the cold night air with that man until the wee hours." Coming in behind her sister, Vera shook a knobby finger at her sister and pulled out a chair. With a superior harrumph, she sat down and smoothed a napkin over her sensible tweed skirt.

"Now, sister," Violet said gently, for she seldom responded in kind, at least in Liz's experience. "We weren't 'sitting out until the wee hours.' It was just for an hour or so in that lovely gazebo. I haven't seen Stefan in ages. We had a lot of catching up to do."

"I can't imagine how much 'catching up' there could be. You've been calling each other long distance like the telephone was going out of existence."

Violet covered a second sneeze and gave Liz a doleful look. "It's just my hay fever. All the buds coming out." She gave a girlish giggle. "'The darling buds of May,' as Mr. Shakespeare would say."

Liz hid a smile and added hot, crisp waffles to the platter. Vera clearly saw herself as Violet's protector, thinking her sister somewhat naïve. Perhaps Violet was, but she was also charming and sweet. *Violet and Stefan have been keeping in touch. Good for them.* They had met at the Olde Mansion Inn on a previous visit. Stefan was a widower, and Violet was just what he needed.

Vera shook her head at her sister, causing her short gray curls to bob like small springs.

"May I offer you a waffle?" Liz asked Vera in an attempt to change the subject to something less volatile. "There are fresh strawberries and whipped cream for topping."

"Too much acid in strawberries," Vera declared, rising and sending her napkin tumbling to the floor. "I'll just help myself to cereal there on the sideboard. You do have shredded wheat, don't you? I can't abide all those sweet cereals. 'The more sugar you soak, the quicker you croak,' you know. And I'll need skim milk. The high-fat varieties clog the arteries like wet cement."

Liz managed not to laugh.

"I'd absolutely love a waffle, dear," Violet said grandly. "And the strawberries look heavenly." In an aside to Liz, she whispered, "I'll have the whipped cream too. A double dollop, if you don't mind."

Sarah's entrance with the coffeepot in hand interrupted an objection from Vera, who seemed ready to launch another barb at her sister. Sarah smiled graciously as she poured steaming, aromatic coffee into the sisters' cups. The strings of her Kapp trailed over her white apron, which covered a pastel lavender dress. "Good morning," she said in her gentle way. "I trust you slept well."

Liz slid the requested waffle with toppings onto Violet's plate, and the older woman dug in with great enthusiasm while her sister watched with disdain.

"I slept like a baby, dear," Violet cooed, touching her napkin to her lips.

"I did not!" Vera said testily. "If people would adhere to respectable hours, we all could get the requisite hours of sleep we need."

"Sister—"

"Oh, I don't mean you this time," Vera interrupted. "You were late enough, but that woman in the Sunset Room! Rushing in, then out again, then blowing back in after midnight." She quickly dropped her voice because the sound of footsteps on the stairs announced the possible arrival of the woman in question.

So, Penny was out late—again, Liz thought. Sarah said she had gone out right after checking in on Monday. And on Tuesday, she hadn't gotten up for breakfast. One would think after a long day at work, she would want a good night's rest. Was she renewing old acquaintances? Where was she going? *Mind your own business*, Liz told herself firmly. She turned to welcome Penny Stryker the way a gracious hostess should.

Penny paused in the doorway and placed one bejeweled hand on her hip. "Something smells delicious!" She was dazzling in a turquoise suit with a long, slim skirt and her trademark high heels. Her platinum hair swung as she surveyed each of the diners—or perhaps she was giving them a chance to see her.

"Good morning, Miss Stryker," Sarah said politely, extending a hand to invite Penny into the room. "Will you have coffee? We also have juice—cranberry, grape, and orange."

From her place behind the table where she was making fresh waffles, Liz greeted Penny and listed the breakfast options. She had predetermined not to be dazzled by Penny, but found herself hardly able to look away from the woman, who was like some exotic bird. Liz waited as Penny's gaze swept over the array of breakfast items. Her false eyelashes were so thick and spiky that it almost appeared that two large spiders had taken up residence on her face.

"Just black coffee and a slice of toast for me. No, don't trouble yourself, Liz. I'll get it." She lifted a piece of wheat bread and placed it delicately in the toaster next to the tray of breads. She looked directly at Liz and waggled her heavily ringed fingers. "No butter for me. We girls have to watch our figures, don't we?"

Liz managed not to roll her eyes. "Did you find everything all right? I hope you were comfortable."

"Thank you, yes," Penny acknowledged. "I'm glad to see the Olde Mansion Inn is still thriving after all these years."

It was a toss-up whether Penny meant that as a compliment or not. Then again, it could have been a shot aimed to remind Liz that Pleasant Creek had been Penny's home before Liz had arrived. She prepared to excuse herself to do something in the kitchen. She didn't know what that something would be, but anything to get her out of the dining room. She'd scrub her counters with a toothbrush if she had to.

Just then, Sadie came in. "Morning, folks. I thought I smelled waffles," she said, standing next to Liz. She cast a hungry eye at the mound of bright-red strawberries and dish of hand-whipped cream. "Something told me I should open Sew Welcome early this morning."

"I'll make up a fresh waffle just for you. Please sit down and have a cup of coffee." Liz hesitated, for Penny had turned around from the tray of bread to survey the newcomer with a startled look that made her eyes even bigger. "I don't believe you've met the new public relations consultant who's also a guest here. Sadie Schwarzentruber, this is Penny Stryker."

Penny recovered from her initial jolt of surprise and inclined her head like a condescending monarch. "Pleased to meet you."

"Sadie co-owns the fabric shop located here at the inn," Liz explained. She looked from Penny to Sadie, whose eyebrows had drawn closer together beneath her sharp blue eyes.

Penny mumbled something like, "How nice," and, averting her eyes, proceeded to the table.

"Do come and sit with us," Violet said to Penny. "I absolutely love that color on you. It's so becoming."

"Thank you," Penny said, easing herself into a chair across from Violet.

"And Sadie, you come sit with us too," Violet added. "Vera and I are both so anxious to see what's new in your shop. We're so sorry we haven't made it in yet this time."

Sadie drew her gaze away from Penny, but the frown remained on her features. She was well-acquainted with the Holmes sisters, who had frequented Sew Welcome on prior visits. Vera had already volunteered to lend her "expertise" for the town market event.

The conversation continued as Liz poured herself another cup of coffee and sat down. Penny raved about the "quaint" old quilts the Amish women made and how she simply must purchase at least one before they were all snatched up.

Vera's eyes registered disapproval, but she said, "I understand you're from Pleasant Creek."

"A very long time ago," Penny said, dabbing her lips with a napkin. "But yes, we lived on the east side of town in that lovely old three-story house with the columns in front. It was only for a few years. My parents moved to Cape Cod—bought a new house on a hill facing the sea. But I always remembered this charming little town." She made a wide arc with her arms. "So much has changed since those days, but when this job opened up, I thought it would be a perfect opportunity to reconnect." She took a sip of coffee. "And who would have thought that handsome Jackson Cross would be so successful in business and become the mayor! Why, you could have knocked me over with a feather."

The expression on Sadie's face said she would like to be holding the feather—or perhaps something heavier. Liz mused that Sadie might have known Penny as a high schooler, but no doubt she was much changed since her teen years.

"Sadie has lived here all her life, Penny," Liz said, trying to lighten the mood. "She might know your aunt. What's her name?"

Penny delicately nibbled a corner of her toast. Her nose tilted up as though something was distasteful. "Margaret Carstairs. She's my mother's sister. But I doubt many folks knew her. She's originally from New York, where she moved in very elite circles."

Liz thought she felt the heat of Sadie's anger—to which her friend had every right. The comment was insulting, as if Sadie couldn't possibly move in the same circles as Penny's uppity family.

Liz wasn't surprised that Sadie finished her waffle and coffee in record time and said she had to get into the shop. Penny declared that she, too, had to run, and with a great flourish, she swept out of the dining room. The Holmes sisters also excused themselves. Sarah and Liz exchanged resigned looks and began to clear away the remains of breakfast.

————————— ///////////////////////////// —————————

"I need a diversion," Liz had said when she popped her head back into Sew Welcome later that afternoon. She had not been able to stop wondering about Reece. And if she were completely honest with herself, she needed something to take her mind off Penny's return to Pleasant Creek. Had Jackson known who the newly hired consultant was? Maybe been involved in the hiring process? If so, what had he been thinking? Was he just interested in helping an old acquaintance—or was it something more?

So it was that Liz found herself once again heading toward Reston. Sadie had quickly agreed to ride with her, leaving Mary Ann in charge of the shop.

"You shouldn't go alone. You never know what you're getting into," Sadie said. "I didn't like the looks of that Benedikt Hoffman. Besides, can you trust anyone with the name Benedikt? Makes me think of Benedict Arnold. Why would his parents stick him with a traitor's name?"

"Perhaps because the name doesn't have the same kind of history to the Amish that it does to us since they didn't participate in the Revolutionary War," Liz said. "After we met him, I did a search on his name. It means 'blessed.' And remember, he goes by Ben."

"Wise choice," Sadie said. "But he seemed awfully eager to get rid of us, so I don't trust him no matter what his name means. And whoever that woman in the kitchen was, she wasn't Amish. Did you see any sign of a buggy on that farm?"

"It's odd, but there's probably a good explanation. I just want to make sure Reece is all right and see if there's anything I can do to help."

"That's you, Liz. Always ready to see the good side of everyone." Sadie patted her arm. "You certainly don't deserve the digs of that so-called 'consultant' I met today. 'Quaint old quilts' indeed! Pretending some special relationship with Jackson and flaunting her jewelry like a prima donna."

"Well, at least she brought our permit for the market," Liz said. "And you must admit she has bold taste in clothes."

"Nonsense. They're completely over the top for the occasion. She's like some kind of ridiculous peacock," Sadie said reproachfully. "And I sure don't remember her from as long ago as she claims. Of course she probably looked a lot different when she was in high school. Still, there's something familiar about her. I don't mean long-ago familiar. I've seen that face somewhere more recently."

The clouds had hung heavily throughout the morning. Now as they turned onto the road leading to the Hoffman farm, a drizzling rain fell, making the road slippery and obscuring Liz's vision despite her windshield wipers going full tilt. Trees and bushes shrouded the road.

"Somebody should cut down some of this brush," Sadie observed.

The gate was again open, and they proceeded up the drive to

the clearing and pulled up close to the house. Beyond the house, the barn and outbuildings lay cloaked in mist. An eight-foot board fence surrounded one of the larger sheds, and there was evidence of wheel ruts in the ground near it. There were no workers in the rain-soaked fields, and everything appeared sinister and foreboding in the gloom.

"This is definitely not Sunnybrook Farm," Sadie said. "And from what you've told me, Reece is no Rebecca."

They proceeded to the door, shivering in the unexpected chill that came with the rain. As Liz pulled up the hood of her anorak, her eye caught a slight movement in an upper-story window. She squinted to see clearly, but a filmy curtain hung over it. Was someone watching from that window? Then the curtain fell, as though some hand had suddenly released it. She exchanged a nervous glance with Sadie and rapped on the door.

"Maybe no one's home," Sadie whispered. "I don't hear any activity, and I don't see lights—kerosene or otherwise."

Thirty seconds passed with no sound from inside the house, and then suddenly, the door opened. In the light of one dim lamp, a tall woman with a grooved, stony face peered at them through slate-colored eyes. Her hair was gray and straight, tucked untidily around prominent ears. She wore a long-sleeved brown dress, buttoned down the front, and a gingham apron around her waist. She was thin as a pencil. "Yes, what is it?" she asked in a flat, gravelly voice.

"Hello," Liz said, swallowing her surprise. "Are you Mrs. Hoffman?"

"I am not," she responded shortly and stood looking at them, without offering to say who she was.

"I'm Liz Eckardt. I'm the one who brought Miss Hoffman's suitcase here on Monday evening," Liz explained. "Reece and I got our luggage mixed up on our flight to Indianapolis. I wanted to say hello to her. Is she home?" Liz felt an unusual dryness in her throat.

"I'm sorry, but the young lady is not well enough to see anyone."

Liz licked her lips. "I-I see," she stammered, unnerved by the elderly woman's abruptness. *So much for Amish hospitality.* "I wonder, is Mr. Hoffman in? We spoke the other day when we visited, and I thought perhaps—"

"Mr. Hoffman is busy. He can't see you now." The woman's manner was brusque.

"We've come all the way from Pleasant Creek," Sadie put in crisply. "Do you know when Mr. Hoffman *will* be available? Or the young lady's grandmother, whom I understand she came expressly to visit."

The woman's eyes briefly connected with Sadie's and flickered. "I'm sure I do not, but I will let them know you came. Lovina Hoffman is away for an extended period. I believe she is caring for an ailing relative. I am merely the housekeeper. I know nothing more." After an uncomfortable few seconds, she added in a dismissive tone, "We are very busy here. I'm sorry." Stepping back in her low-heeled slippers, she began to close the door.

"I'd like to call Miss Hoffman," Liz said. "People recover faster when they know others are thinking of them. Is there a number where she can be reached?"

The housekeeper shook her head. "I'm sorry. If you care to leave your number, I will see that she gets it."

Though Liz had already given Reece her card with her number, she reached into her purse and drew out a second card, which she handed to the housekeeper. The door closed in their faces before they had time to say anything more.

As they walked away from the farmhouse, Liz turned to look over her shoulder at the window where she thought someone might have been watching.

But she must have been wrong. Nothing moved behind the filmy curtain. Liz let out a weary breath. That she was *persona non grata* at the Hoffman home was abundantly clear. What remained a mystery was why?

7

The first three days of the week vanished on fleet wings. Liz had been playing catch-up since returning from the conference in Maine, and the suitcase mix-up and two visits to the Hoffman farm had only added to the workload—and to the confusion. Liz couldn't help thinking something wasn't quite right there, and from time to time Reece's face appeared like a chronic pop-up ad in her mind, demanding attention.

But the inn needed her focus more, including the new guests who had arrived just after supper the night before. Karl and June Anderson from Chicago were celebrating their thirtieth wedding anniversary, and Liz had gone to great lengths to make sure the Heirloom Room looked its gracious best. She had carefully laundered the hand-tatted lace pillows that accented the antique blue-and-white coverlet on the four-poster bed. She hoped they would enjoy the cushy contemporary sofa, antique chest and tables, and the early-1900s Tiffany lamps. As a special touch, she had prepared a congratulatory fruit basket and set it on the mantel above the finely carved fireplace.

"Thank you for everything, Ms. Eckardt," June said warmly when she and her husband were enjoying coffee hour in the cozy sitting room that Thursday.

"It's my pleasure, and please call me Liz. We're so glad you could join us."

"So are we. These scones are so flaky and tasty," June said in a cultured voice. Her gray linen slacks and pale-green blouse were of fine quality. She had light-green eyes and short copper-colored hair almost artistically streaked with silver.

"The scones are Sarah's handiwork," Liz said, nodding to the young woman, who was refilling Violet's cup with the special Assam tea that was popular with many guests. "She has a magic touch with pastries."

"Welcome to the Olde Mansion Inn," Violet said with a warm smile. Liz got the impression that after several visits Violet felt a certain ownership and wanted everyone to relish the merits of her favorite bed-and-breakfast. "I'm Violet Holmes," the older woman added after taking another bite of her scone. "And this is my sister, Vera."

Sitting primly next to her sister, Vera nodded. She cleared her throat and folded her hands in her lap, as though prepared to give a speech. The lines around her mouth softened a bit, which made her sometimes sour face almost pretty.

The sound of sharp raps on the wood floor drew everyone's eye to the door. Penny Stryker's four-inch heels announced her unexpected arrival. She was wearing a black straw hat as big as a sombrero, which was adorned with a huge turquoise rose, the final accent for her designer suit that had wowed Violet at breakfast.

"I do hope I'm not late. I understand your coffee hours are quite magnificent, Liz, although I prefer tea in the afternoon," she warbled. "I'm making the rounds of all the institutions that service the public, just to make sure we're putting our best foot forward in Pleasant Creek. I'm sure you have all the proper documents here at the Olde Mansion Inn." She scrutinized the sitting room. "Ah, and I see we have new guests. How very nice." She flashed the Andersons a quick, if penetrating, glance and took an empty chair next to Violet.

Sarah quickly poured tea into a delicate teacup for Penny and offered her a plate of scones. The conversation in the room had stilled. Liz realized that Penny enjoyed stunning audiences with her flamboyance. From Violet, she received a beaming smile. Vera sent a scowl in her direction and then turned to address the Andersons.

"I understand you are from Chicago. My sister and I live in Louisville. We had an aunt who lived in Chicago, on the west side." She pursed her lips slightly and waited for a response.

June nodded, smiling. "Yes, we are," she said and turned to her husband, who had not spoken and appeared distracted.

Karl was handsome with silver hair and a well-trimmed mustache. There was a dignity about him as well as an air of success, but these qualities seemed muted at the moment. A newspaper lay flattened on his knees, but he wasn't reading it, and his tea sat cooling in front of him as he stared through the sitting room window. He looked up at his wife's prodding, and Liz saw worry lines around his mouth and kindly eyes.

"How do you do?" he said in a rusty baritone. "Karl Anderson and my wife, June." He nodded politely to the Holmes sisters and fell silent.

"We own an antiques business on the north side," June offered. "We're taking a few days to celebrate our anniversary. Our thirtieth," she added, touching the sleeve of her husband's sport jacket, which Liz recognized as a Canali. The item sold for more than $1,000 in a Neiman Marcus catalog she'd recently seen. He wore it with casual elegance over light wool slacks. Liz also knew from the address on their registration that their upscale shop was in Chicago's Gold Coast area. They'd told her they dealt in high-end collectibles, art, and jewelry.

"How very interesting," Penny mused, pinching off a dainty bite of scone. "What is the name of your store?" she asked, lightly fluttering her eyelashes.

"The Golden Leopard," Karl replied wearily and folded the leaf of newspaper on his lap as though he might be preparing to leave the room. The lines in his forehead deepened. Whatever was troubling him was likely related to his business, and he probably had no wish to discuss it among the ladies gathered in the sitting room. He sat back in the chair.

"It's been a fine venture for several years," June offered, looking slightly annoyed at her husband's diffidence. "We've been in business for twenty-nine years—we started it just after we were married—and I don't mind saying we've done quite well for ourselves." The pride on her face was evident.

"Do you have children?" Liz asked, then took a bite of her own scone. Delicious, as always. Sarah's scones were so rich and satisfying, they didn't even need butter. *Though a little of that Amish-made raspberry jam wouldn't hurt*, she thought. She reached for the jar and spoon on the tray and spread a bit of the sweet, sticky substance on her pastry.

"We do," June said, her face lighting up. "We have two sons, and both work in the business with us."

Karl just sat there, staring at the doorway, but Vera nodded approvingly. "I think that's wonderful. So few children are interested in following in their parents' footsteps these days."

"But," Violet said, her voice soft, almost timid. "*Children* should be free to follow their own paths, shouldn't they?" Her cheeks took on a becoming blush.

Vera glared at her sister.

June smiled and didn't comment. "One studied philosophy at college, and the other majored in something called sports theory. And they both came back to the business voluntarily a couple of years ago."

Liz shook her head. "I don't know about sports theory, whatever that is, but I imagine paying philosopher's jobs are difficult to come by."

June let out a musical laugh. "Their educations were expensive, but we could afford it, and I'm glad they got to study what they wanted. And I'm even happier they've come back to us."

Liz glanced at Karl. Not even talk of his sons brought him out of his distracted silence.

With a sidelong glance at her husband, June told them that their sons had urged their parents to get away for a few days. "Karl didn't really want to leave the store, but he also didn't want to disappoint me on our anniversary." She looked at him expectantly, but he maintained his silence, so she continued. "We've had some trouble lately. We've lost quite a few valuable items—that is, they were stolen. It hasn't been good for our bottom line."

"I'm so sorry," Violet breathed, grasping the purple beads at her neck in dismay.

"We're not the only ones." Karl roused himself, straightening slightly in his chair. "There have been several thefts in our area that the police are investigating. They've traced some of the stolen items to this part of Indiana."

Beans, who was asleep near Penny and clearly dreaming, let out a low growl as his legs started to twitch. One of his paws jerked out and hit Penny's leg. There was a clank of china, and Liz turned to see Penny spill hot tea into her lap. "Oh!" she shrieked, dislodging her huge hat, which flopped on the floor. "My skirt!"

At the same moment, Beans sprang to life with a grunt. He crushed the hat in his eagerness to snatch the remains of Penny's scone, which had also fallen to the floor.

Liz scrambled up, and Sarah hurried over with a tea towel as Penny began to complain loudly. Liz ordered Beans to his bed and hurried to help, issuing sincere apologies. Penny's skirt bore a telltale dark stain. In the general hubbub, coffee hour ended and the other guests slipped away to escape the unpleasant situation.

Liz led Penny into the kitchen. "We'll get the worst of the stain out right away. I'm terribly sorry. Did it burn you?"

"Of course it did," she snapped. "That tea was boiling hot! And what was that animal doing in there? He's ruined my hat!"

Sarah stepped into the fray and picked up the hat with its deflated flower. She brushed and smoothed it, trying to restore its shape as Liz worked to calm the offended lady. "Beans didn't mean any harm. He just got excited."

"I think your hat will be fine now," Sarah said in her soothing voice. She held it toward Penny, who snatched it from her with an angry toss of her head.

Penny glared at Liz. "Surely you are aware of the rules!" she said. Before Liz could respond, Penny continued, "Live animals must be excluded from within the food service preparation and storage areas. That's article 54, section D of the town regulatory code."

Beans peeked out from under the table and sidled up to Liz. "Sit, Beans," Liz ordered. The dog sat, but continued to stare up at Penny, tongue hanging out, as if waiting for her to drop another crumb of scone. Normally his silly expression brought a smile to an irritated guest's face, but Penny was having none of it and continued to scowl. "That creature is disgusting."

Liz felt her training as a lawyer kick in. Who did the woman think she was? The health department? "The sitting room isn't a prep or a storage area," she said quietly. Besides, Beans was clean and generally very well-behaved. People loved him. Well, most people.

"It's part of my job to ensure that all establishments that serve the public are properly licensed and operated," Penny said, drawing herself up to her full height. She clutched her hat over her soaked skirt and glared down at Beans with complete disdain. "That animal certainly shouldn't be here in the kitchen, where I assume you *do* prep and store food. I'll be making a note of it in my report." She stormed out of the room, the heels of her shoes clacking on the floor.

Liz and Sarah stood still until the footsteps died away, then turned to each other, speechless.

Finally, Sarah's lips started to twitch.

"What's so funny?" Liz asked.

Sarah's face split into a broad grin. "Her face when Beans squashed her hat."

Remembering the expression of shock and outrage on Penny's face, Liz had to agree, and she and Sarah laughed without restraint as Beans sat at their feet, giving them his doggy grin.

———————— *///////////////////////////////* ————————

"I really need coffee and some of Mary Ann's comfort pie," Liz said when she arrived in Sew Welcome for a meeting of the Material Girls in the early evening. "You've no idea what kind of day I had." She dropped down on a chair in the cozy back room of the shop and inhaled the fragrance of vanilla roast coffee brewing.

Mary Ann got up to fill Liz's cup and serve her a generous slice of strawberry-rhubarb pie. "It's the first of our rhubarb crop," she said, smiling. "And it's surprisingly sweet with the strawberries, but there's still a little tanginess." She smiled at Liz, brown eyes sympathetic.

Sadie pursed her lips and gave Liz a knowing glance. "Oh, we might just have some idea what kind of day you had. The Holmes sisters came in this afternoon."

"Ah," said Liz, releasing a sigh. "Unfortunately, the ladies saw the whole thing. I feel really bad about that. I hate having our guests witness an unpleasant scene."

"If you ask me, Vera and Violet found it more entertaining than a comedy matinee." Sadie folded her arms over her bright-purple sweater, lips twitching slightly. "Did Beans really step on that snooty lady's hat?"

Liz felt herself redden. "Smashed it good and proper," she said dismally. "And hot tea got spilled all over her skirt."

"Vera says it was Penny's own fault," Sadie said staunchly. "And I'm sure it was."

"She is a fancy dresser," Opal said, looking up from her knitting. "My daughter saw her downtown. Said she seemed like a page out of a fashion magazine. If she hadn't been in a hurry to get Maddy to her dance class, she would have asked her where she got her hair done."

"That skirt may never be the same," Liz said, taking a large bite of pie. "And she said she's going to report us to the town. Apparently Beans is a code violation."

"Poor guy was probably scared to death," Caitlin said. She brushed a lock of bright-red hair out of her eyes. Caitlin, a nurse in her twenties, had a rescued greyhound pup named Kelly that she adored. She'd told the Material Girls that when she went to work at the hospital, she left the television tuned to the animal channel so Kelly wouldn't be lonely.

"I think he was more interested in getting a bit of scone than he was frightened," Liz said. She sighed. "Penny apparently views herself as some kind of superhero who's going to solve all the town's problems. I did some checking up on her earlier today, just a quick Internet search. She apparently worked at a publicity firm in Chicago before coming here. I called, but they wouldn't divulge any information beyond confirming that she'd been employed there."

"It was worth a try. She's just jealous of you because of Jackson," Naomi put in. "You told me she looked daggers at you when she saw you with him the other night. Don't worry. Penelope Stryker is just a temporary consultant for special events. She's not actually in a place to get you in trouble. Jackson will keep her in line if she tries anything."

Liz felt better, as she always did, in the company of her friends. She threaded her needle to help with one of the quilts that would be sold at the town market. There was nothing like getting into a project that required diligence and concentration to refocus the mind, and there was nothing like the almost meditative movement of the needle to calm it. When she quilted, Liz was always in awe of how the craft made her feel connected to generations of quilters who had come before her.

"The Andersons seem like a very nice couple," Mary Ann offered. "Mrs. Anderson dropped in earlier today and bought three of our best quilts."

"They're celebrating their anniversary," Liz explained as she made a few stitches, following the stenciled outline on the fabric. "But Mr. Anderson is preoccupied with the robbery at their antiques store."

"I read about that," Mary Ann said. "Several high-end stores were robbed. Since the robberies happened in the same area and the same kinds of items were taken, the police think the incidents are related."

Liz leaned forward in her chair. "Well, being robbed is not a happy way to celebrate your anniversary. I put the Andersons in the Heirloom Room and tried to make things special for them. But after the fiasco at coffee hour, they may wish they'd gone somewhere else to mark their special day."

"Oh, I wouldn't worry too much about it," Sadie put in. "Like Naomi said, Jackson will rein Penny in if she gets up too high on her horse."

Liz would have liked to tell Jackson just what a pill Penny had been today, but how would that sound? Like a green-eyed, insecure adolescent tattling to the adults about a problem she should handle herself. Penny was probably all sweetness and light when official eyes were upon her, but she'd reveal her true colors eventually—wouldn't she? *Besides, I don't know her story.* That's what her mother used to say when Liz criticized someone. Liz didn't know what had happened in Penny's life to cause such behavior.

As she had so many times in the years since her mother's death, Liz wished she could talk to her mom. Whatever experiences came, Liz would remember the wise principles her Amish-raised mother had taught her—not that Liz had known her mother had been raised Amish at the time. Just remembering those things wasn't the same as pouring out her heart to her mother, with her kind face and understanding eyes. Liz sighed and finished the last stitches in the row she was working on.

The hours passed swiftly, and the Material Girls began packing up their work. It was almost eight o'clock when Liz's cell phone vibrated suddenly in the pocket of her jeans. She checked the screen. No name. The number was unfamiliar, but it was preceded by a nearby area code. Usually she let unknown calls go to voice mail, but this time she decided to pick up.

"Hello?" she said.

There was no reply, even when she repeated the greeting twice more. But she could hear someone's shuddering breath. She was about to click off when a woman's anxious voice asked, "Ms. Eckardt? Liz?"

"Yes, this is Liz," she said.

The caller spoke in a whisper, as if her throat was sore. "I need help—"

"Who is this?" Liz asked, alarm rising. "Who's calling?"

Seconds of silence elapsed, and then the hushed voice said, "Please come—"

"What's wrong? Where are you?"

There was a click, and the line went dead.

Liz gaped at the phone.

The voice had been familiar. Liz racked her brain trying to think who might be calling her in such a troubled state. Reece? The voice was similar, but Liz couldn't be sure. She hadn't spoken to the young woman enough, and it had been three busy days since she'd heard Reece's voice. Should she call the police? And if it was an emergency, why hadn't Reece—or whoever it was—called 911? She redialed the caller's number, but there was no answer.

"Everything okay?" Sadie asked.

Liz bit her lip, a chill traveling up her spine. "I don't know," she said softly. She met Sadie's gaze. "Feel like going on a rescue mission?"

8

"Are you sure we should be doing this?" Sadie asked when they were settled inside Liz's Acura and once more on the road to Reston. "I'm always up for an adventure, but you don't know that it was Reece calling. It could have been anyone."

Liz frowned. "I know." She had made many friends in Pleasant Creek and had found relatives that she hadn't known existed. She couldn't think of anyone else who might be in some kind of trouble and would think to call her. "She sounded desperate," Liz said. "She spoke so softly I could barely hear her, but I'm almost sure it was her."

Had Reece's illness worsened and there was no one at home to help her? Twice Liz had gone to see her at the farm and been told Reece was too ill to see her, even though Ben had at first indicated it was nothing more than a headache. On the second visit, the housekeeper had said Reece was still not well enough to see anyone, which meant it was worse than just a headache. So maybe that was it. The young woman's condition had deteriorated and she needed assistance. For some reason, she had not been able to reach Ben or the housekeeper or the absent grandmother.

Liz's mind reeled at a sudden thought. *Is Reece being held at that farm against her will?* Was that possible? Liz shivered. Her imagination was getting away from her.

"I'm sorry to drag you out so late, but I'm glad you're with me, Sadie."

"Do you think I'd let you go traipsing off to that farm alone, especially at this hour? You probably should have called Jackson. You never know what people are up to these days."

"She sounded like she needed help right away," Liz replied. "And you were available. Sorry."

"Never mind," Sadie said. "Mary Ann will lock up, and your guests will be fine for a little while, even a certain disagreeable one. Speaking of disagreeable guests, I bet after she calms down from her little hissy fit, Penny will be too embarrassed to show her face for a while. Any decent person would be. And I'm sure I'm not the only one who's okay with that."

Liz sighed with weariness. It had indeed been a long day.

"I'm getting to know this route by heart," Sadie said.

"Maybe you can drive it in your Jeep sometime. Have you had any updates on that?" Liz asked.

"No one's seen hide nor hair of it. You'd think it would have surfaced by now. I've been searching for it everywhere. Well, not everywhere. But unless it's in some other county miles from here, that car should have turned up."

"I know how much it means to you, Sadie," Liz said. "I'm sorry."

"When it comes down to it, it's just a car. My insurance will cover it, and life goes on." Sadie let her breath out in a long stream. "But it makes me mad! And the skunk who stole it probably hasn't lost an hour of sleep."

"A conscience can be a real liability if you're a thief." Liz slowed as a deer darted across the road.

"You're right about that," Sadie said. "Oh, there's our turn. They sure don't want to advertise their place. If you didn't know it was there, you'd pass right by it, especially at night."

They turned onto the narrow dirt road where trees shrouded both sides, shutting out any light the moon might afford. The iron gate that had been open on earlier visits was now set across the entrance. It was comprised of two crossed bars, which a pedestrian could easily step over, but her Acura wasn't going any farther.

"Apparently Reece's grandmother values her privacy," Liz said.

"But you know that's not really the Amish way. They're quiet and keep to themselves, but hospitality is important," Sadie said. "The only fences you usually see on Amish farms are to enclose livestock, not to bar visitors. Maybe it's a late addition, something Benedikt installed." She looked from the gate to Liz. "Obviously we're not wanted here. But Reece may be in trouble."

Liz put the car in park at the gate and considered. "I suppose the smart thing to do would be to go into town and find the local sheriff. Let him investigate." *But tell him what? That a call for help* might *have come from this farm?*

"We could do that," Sadie mused, examining the fence. "Or we could step over that fence, walk up to the house, and put our minds to rest about that young woman."

Their course set, they exited the car and clambered over the gate. The driveway seemed longer than before. Liz couldn't tell if it was because of the darkness or because they were walking this time. Finally, they reached their destination.

The farm lay silent, except for the house where a dull light on the lower floor shone behind curtains. There were no outdoor lights, and it was difficult to see more than a few feet ahead. It was hardly the time to come calling, especially when a closed gate should have been sufficient to deter guests.

Nevertheless, Liz and Sadie walked up the path to the house, heads high, and knocked with determination. Yes, it was after nine o'clock, but they had good reason to interrupt whatever was going on inside. Several seconds passed, and there was no sound from within. Somewhere beyond the house and barn came the barking of a dog, but no one appeared to greet them, human or animal. "Maybe no one is home," Liz suggested. "Or maybe Reece is too ill to answer."

Sadie shuffled her feet. "This is crazy," she said. "Where is everyone?"

Suddenly the door opened, though they had heard no footsteps approaching. The housekeeper, tall and angular, stood on the threshold, her features screwed into a puzzled frown. She wore an identical dress and apron to the one they had seen the previous day, and her feet were thrust into a pair of flat brown slippers. "You again," she said with unconcealed surprise. "What do you want at this hour?"

Liz judged her to be in her early sixties. She stood straight, holding knobby, red hands rigidly at her sides. The furrows in her face and dull eyes indicated a life of hard work and discontent. The left eye, smaller than the right, drooped oddly beside a prominent nose, which might have given her face an aristocratic appearance except for the large ears that stuck out too far.

"I've had a call from Reece," Liz said. "We wouldn't have breached your privacy by climbing over your gate, but Reece said she needed help."

The housekeeper looked at Liz and then at Sadie with wide, unflinching eyes, but her hands opened and closed rapidly at her sides. "I assure you the girl is asleep in her room. She is not in need of your help. She is receiving the best care we can give her." She raised her large nose, flaring the nostrils. The gesture indicated that she was especially not in need of help from the likes of them.

"But she called me."

"Whoever called you, it could not have been Reece."

"But . . ." Liz floundered. "If I could just see her and make certain she's all right—"

"Mr. Hoffman ordered that his cousin was not to be disturbed. As I told you previously, she has been ill. The doctor has instructed that she is to be kept quiet."

"She called and asked us to come." Sadie tried to push her way inside, but the housekeeper held the door firm and looked Sadie up and down.

"I'm sure you are mistaken. I'm very sorry, but I have my orders." The thin woman began to shove the door closed, but Sadie stood her ground on the threshold.

Liz's heart pounded. She took a deep breath and shifted into Lawyer Liz mode. "Perhaps we could just see for ourselves that she's all right. We won't disturb her long, and then we'll be on our way." The woman's unyielding posture and cold eyes served to make Liz more determined. "I must insist on seeing her."

"Is there a problem?" Benedikt Hoffman appeared behind the housekeeper. He was dressed in a white shirt with sleeves rolled up to the elbows and a pair of gray slacks—definitely not farming attire. His light, curly hair was tousled in the front, as though he had been out on a windy day. A pencil was lodged above his right ear. The gentleman farmer going over the estate accounts? Eyes the color of coal peered at Liz. The effect was startling—and more than a little unnerving. *Like everything else about this place.*

"I'm sorry to disturb you, sir," the housekeeper said. "These ladies say your cousin phoned asking for help."

"Is that so?" he asked seriously, eyes mildly curious in his handsome face. He switched places with the housekeeper.

"I told them that she was asleep in her room and that she does not need assistance."

"Thank you, Mrs. Steele. I'll take care of this," he told her. "What can I do for you, ladies?"

Mrs. Steele? There's an apt name. "Someone I believe to be Reece called me about an hour ago," Liz explained again. "My friend and I came right away to make sure she's all right."

"Please, come in," Ben said with a smile. He stood back and gestured inside with a well-groomed hand. "It's good of you to be concerned about my cousin. We all are. She gets confused when she's in the grip of one of her headaches. She's never quite herself when she has them." He ushered them into a small sitting room with a plain beige couch, a rocker, and two straight-backed chairs. No adornments hung on the walls or decorated the simple table. Liz could imagine Reece's grandmother rocking before the fire in this typical Amish sitting room, which seemed now cold and empty, unlike the other Amish homes she'd visited.

"Confused?" Liz repeated. "Not herself? I don't understand."

"Well," he said graciously, "You don't know her well, since you've only recently met, but when her migraines flare up they can last for days and be quite debilitating."

Liz held his gaze. Was Ben saying that Reece's headaches rendered her incompetent somehow? She knew migraines could be terrible, could send the suffering person to bed, unable to stand any light at all. Maybe Reece's muddled her brain somehow. Ben was right. Liz didn't know Reece, not really.

Ben turned to speak to Mrs. Steele, who had followed them, fumbling with her apron. "Go up and tell Reece she has company. It's all right to wake her. We mustn't keep these dear ladies waiting after they drove all this way just to check on Reece." Inclining his head to Sadie, he added, "Let my cousin know it's Ms. Eckardt and Ms. . . . ?"

"Schwarzentruber. Sadie Schwarzentruber," Liz finished for him.

The man bowed slightly in deference to Sadie and turned back to Liz with an attentive smile. He gave the impression of being completely at ease and in control.

"Mr. Hoffman—" Liz began.

"It's Ben, remember?" he corrected her gently. He gave her a charming smile. "Now that you've been to this home on three occasions, you should at least call me by my first name."

"I understand Reece's grandmother is away," Liz said. "Do you expect her back soon?" It was a bold question. After all, what right did she have to know the family's business?

But Ben seemed unperturbed, though something in the dark eyes flashed briefly. "That's right. Our grandmother is one of those salt-of-the-earth people who feels an obligation to everyone on the planet. The Amish are that way. Well, I suppose you know that, with all the Amish around Pleasant Creek," he said, putting his hands into his pockets. Liz realized Mrs. Steele must have told him about the last time Liz and Sadie had turned up on the doorstep. "I've been holding down the fort for her while she's taking care of a sick woman in Fillmore County. We don't know when she'll get back. She's not one for using the phone."

Fillmore County. That was quite a distance by horse and buggy, but maybe only an hour or so by car. Reece could easily have made the trip to visit her grandmother several times over. If she were well enough, of course. Or Ben could have taken her. Liz's mind reeled with questions and surmises, all the while taking in Ben Hoffman's confident demeanor and his considerable charm.

"Ah, here's Reece now."

Liz followed Ben's gaze to the stairway. Mrs. Steele descended, and behind her came the young woman Liz remembered from the plane. Her steps on the stairs were slow but steady, and she stood tall and regal in a long black skirt. The top two buttons of her yellow top were open as though she had dressed hastily. Her auburn hair hung smoothly to her shoulders and fringed her forehead.

Liz took in the lovely oval of her face, the slight pallor, the tight lips without color. She seemed only slightly disoriented, as though she had been sleeping. Reece observed her guests, then turned her eyes down as she focused on moving to the bottom of the stairs.

Ben went to her and took her arm. "You okay, Reece?" he asked. He helped her into the living room. "These ladies from Pleasant Creek are here to see you. You remember Ms. Eckardt? She said you were on a plane to Indianapolis together." His mellow voice held a slightly condescending note, as though he might be coaxing a child or someone of diminished capacity.

Reece looked into Liz's eyes. "It's good of you to come." She paused briefly, then added, "Ben said you brought my suitcase. I want to thank you for that." She turned to Ben as though unsure what was expected of her.

"Ms. Eckardt says you called her and asked her to come," Ben prompted. "She seems to think something might be troubling you and that you need help. She's very worried about you."

Reece frowned. "I'm sorry," she said in a voice that was suddenly strong and controlled. "There must be some mistake. I didn't call, and as you can see, I'm fine. I should have called to express my thanks for returning my suitcase, but my head has been giving me fits." She touched her temple. "But I do thank you for your trouble tonight in coming to make sure I'm all right."

Liz stared at the young woman and opened her mouth to protest, but stopped. Something in Reece's eyes begged her to keep her peace.

"There, you see? Nothing to worry about," Ben said. "We are quite capable of caring for my cousin when she has her migraines, and she is feeling much better after a couple days of rest. She's eager to visit her grandmother. We plan to see her tomorrow. I'm grateful for your concern on her behalf. You are truly caring women to drive this far this late to check on the well-being of a person you barely know."

Liz heard Sadie expel a frustrated breath. Liz touched her friend's arm with a steadying hand. "It was the decent thing to do. We are so relieved that Reece is on the mend. We—uh—apologize for the confusion, and for intruding on your hospitality so late at night." She smiled at Reece, Ben, and Mrs. Steele. "We'll just be on our way then." She nudged Sadie toward the door.

Ben walked them out like a gracious host, bid them a charming good night, and closed the door of the strange house.

"Well, that's that, I guess," Sadie said when they were a good distance from the house.

Liz said nothing.

"What?" Sadie prodded.

Liz took a deep breath. "She seems all right, but I'm just not convinced."

"Well, that may be so, and I don't disagree with you. That housekeeper was downright creepy, and I still don't like that Ben character. But I don't see what we can do about it. The girl says she's fine and doesn't need or want any help."

"I know. That's what she said, but did you see her eyes?"

"I'd expect someone suffering from a migraine for several days to look like that."

"It's not just Reece," Liz said. "It's everything about this place. The fields don't look like they're being worked. We haven't seen any farmhands or livestock. And what's with the iron gate across the lane—or that eight-foot wooden fence over there?" She pointed. "It's nearly as high as the building behind it. Like you said, the Amish don't believe in fences, except to hold livestock."

"Clearly Ben Hoffman isn't an Amish farmer."

"I don't think he's a farmer at all," Liz declared. "His hands aren't rough or calloused, and his nails are too clean."

"That's because he has hired workers who go home at night," Sadie said. "We weren't here during working hours the first time or this time. The second time we came, it was pouring rain. Can't work the fields in that kind of weather. Everything just turns to sludge."

"Maybe."

"And again," Sadie said, "I'm not disagreeing with you, just pointing out that there could be other explanations for what we're seeing. And yes, I know that's very unlike me. Mary Ann's the levelheaded one." She chuckled.

They paused under a huge sycamore. They had nearly reached the spot where they'd left the car. "I'd like to know what's inside that building over there. That log fence can't be there just for curb appeal." Here was the Sadie Liz knew and loved.

Liz drew in her breath. "Are you suggesting we circle around and try to find a way in?"

Sadie shrugged and grinned.

"If they see us, they'd be within their rights to have us arrested for trespassing."

"We're not trespassing. Ben Hoffman himself invited us in. He just didn't specify where we were and were not allowed to be. If we just take a little peek around while we're here, maybe we can set our minds at ease."

Sadie's blue eyes glittered in the moonlight, and Liz knew the curiosity bug had bitten her too.

"Fine," Liz said. "We'll keep just inside the tree line and work our way to the side farthest from the house, where we won't be seen."

They moved quietly, pushing through foliage and brush to the sounds of crickets and other night creatures probably best left unidentified. As curious as Liz was, she wished she were back at the Olde Mansion Inn, preparing for a good night's rest in her own comfortable bed. Was she out of her mind snooping on a strange farm, looking for who knew what?

Sadie tugged at her arm. "Hold on a minute." She opened the mammoth purse she always carried and began rummaging through it until she pulled out a six-inch flashlight decorated with a busy floral pattern. Its LED light was surprisingly bright.

"Good," Liz whispered. "Shine it over there. Let's see if there's a way to get inside." She peered around nervously to make sure no one was watching.

"There!" Sadie said, training her flashlight on a crude gate with a simple metal latch.

Liz thrust aside the scrubby bushes growing along the fence. Her arms and hands stung from the scratchy weeds. She was glad she had worn jeans, which protected her legs. She reached up to touch the latch. No padlock, and amazingly, she lifted it with one finger. There couldn't be too big a secret inside if it was left unlocked. She turned to give Sadie a look of triumph, then very gently began to press the gate open.

A terrible snarling and barking erupted in the darkness. A huge animal came tearing around the building and headed straight for them, fangs glistening white in the darkness.

Liz slammed the gate shut, her heart on fire as the dog flung itself against the inside of the fence. "Run, Sadie!" she hissed. "They're sure to hear this ruckus!"

They took off at breakneck speed while the dog lunged at the fence again and again, rattling the gate and barking furiously.

"Who needs a lock with something like that inside the fence?" Liz gasped when they reached the car and jumped in.

"Now I'm more curious than ever about what's inside that building," Sadie said. "What's so big a secret that they need that monster to guard it?"

Liz started the car and threw it into reverse. "I don't know. But we need to find out somehow."

9

The next morning, Liz couldn't get the harrowing experience out of her mind. It had admittedly been a bad idea to go snooping around the fenced-in building after leaving the Hoffmans' door. They should have gone directly home and minded their own business. The whole evening seemed surreal, especially when Reece denied calling for help and insisted that she was fine. In the throes of a migraine, she might have called and later forgotten it. Ben had been courteous, if guarded, and Mrs. Steele was beyond reckoning, the stuff of classic Gothic novels.

Unable to sleep, Liz had surfed the Internet for New York modeling agencies and found them to be as numerous as flies. She'd been about to give up when she hit on the right one. She was even able to view Reece's professional photo online. Liz hadn't really doubted she was a model, based on her appearance and bearing, but she was glad to have confirmation. An images search turned up a few photos of her at various events, but she was certainly no supermodel with unlimited jobs. Still, there were enough that it was possible she was making a living at it. And she'd flown first class, so it seemed to be a good living. Then again, Liz herself had been upgraded. It was possible Reece had been too.

Breakfast went smoothly enough. The Andersons seemed rested, though Karl Anderson once again buried his nose in his newspaper while he sipped his coffee. June chatted with the Holmes sisters about the quilts she had purchased at Sew Welcome.

Violet and Stefan were going to the Indianapolis Zoo, which was one of the most popular attractions in the area. They'd invited Vera to come with them but were met with a firm refusal. Vera said she planned to visit the town historian's display at the courthouse, then spend some time in the shops downtown.

Penny breezed in with no hint of her distress the previous day. She grabbed a piece of dry toast and black coffee, and then glided back out. Liz thought she saw Penny throw a cautious glance around the room as she left again, but she was probably just imagining it with her sleep-deprived mind. *Get a grip, Liz. You've got to stop seeing suspicious things everywhere.*

Liz had been careful to keep Beans out of Penny's way. She stooped down to rub the gentle bulldog's ears, suddenly remembering the dog at the Hoffman farm, who was not nearly as affable. She shivered, recalling the ferocious beast lunging at the fence.

She shook the image away. Today was a beautiful day, yesterday's gloom and dampness gone. She was determined to enjoy it.

Before heading into town, Liz phoned Reece's modeling agency. A harried, professional voice affirmed the young woman was indeed under contract there. "We've been trying to reach her," she said impatiently. Her voice was muffled for a moment as she responded to someone on her end, then she barked into the phone, "Please have her call the agency if she intends to continue her contract with us."

Why hadn't Reece advised her employer of her whereabouts? Was she simply irresponsible? Unconcerned about her next job? Or was there some other reason?

Liz pushed these questions into the back of her mind and drove to the town hall, determined to enjoy the beauty of the bright spring day. The greens—pale lime to dark forest and every shade in between—seemed to explode against the sky. The leaves of elms, maples, and sycamores mingled with blossoming trees in pink, mauve, and white. It dazzled the eye. She cracked her windows to usher in the mild breezes, as well as the whistles and warbles of busy birds.

Shops were being readied for the warm season, windows newly redecorated, planters refreshed. Pleasant Creek citizens showed their community pride by carefully maintaining and regularly improving their properties. Even the town hall, with its flag waving merrily overhead, seemed to have benefited from a face-lift. She parked the car and made her way inside.

She headed toward Jackson's tasteful office. Mindful of the city's budget, Jackson wasn't one to demand a corner office or special perks, even as mayor. She wasn't expected, but his door was open for visitors. Eagerly she headed for the doorway, then stopped short.

Penny sat across from Jackson. She wore a sleeveless blouse of white silk, a crimson skirt, and stiletto heels with straps that crisscrossed fussily around the ankles. She swept back a wave of platinum hair that had fallen across her cheek. Perched on the edge of her chair, the woman was smiling at Jackson, who wore an expression of patient reserve. At the sound of Liz's step, Penny turned, her cherry lips forming a startled *O*.

Jackson got up, a smile lighting his face. "Come on in, Liz. What brings you by?"

His tone was low and unruffled, but Liz thought she saw his color deepen.

"I thought I'd see if you were free for lunch. But if you're busy..."

"Oh," Penny said, also rising and clicking the end of the pen she was holding. "We're all through here. I just had a few teeny little questions, and Jackson was kind enough to answer them for me."

Liz only nodded as Penny swiftly exited with her "teeny little questions." In her wake was a strong scent of some expensive perfume.

Jackson lifted his sport coat from the back of his desk chair and slung it over one shoulder. "Ready if you are," he said, slipping his free arm over her shoulder. "I'm glad you came."

"I didn't mean to interrupt you."

"You are an interruption of the most welcome kind." He closed the office door after them and led her outside into the sunshine. They agreed to walk to The Coffee Cup, one of their favorite lunch spots.

Liz usually had to hurry to keep up with Jackson's long stride, but today he seemed content to stroll at a leisurely pace, and she willed herself to relax as she walked beside him. They threaded their way through the small crowd, greeting friends and neighbors as they went, and found a booth near the back of the restaurant.

The Coffee Cup thrummed with activity, but no background music hampered conversation, and they settled in with their menus. Jackson ordered a mushroom burger with fries. Liz chose a BLT with a side of coleslaw. Both requested raspberry lemonade.

They sipped their drinks quietly for a few moments, and then Jackson cleared his throat. Liz saw his brows furrow slightly.

"Just so you know, when I agreed to her hire, I didn't know she was *that* Penny," he said quietly. "She had a different last name when I knew her years ago."

"Years?" she teased. "I think it may seem like yesterday to her, given her behavior around you. But who can blame her?"

He colored slightly and pushed his fork an inch or so to the left. "I'm sorry if she's giving you trouble, but she seems eager to be helpful."

Liz could argue that last point, but his assurance made her feel better about the issue. She chose to dismiss the whole topic of Penny. She smiled across the table at him. "I don't worry about you, Jackson."

His face broke into a smile. "Good. You have no reason to. Now tell me what you've been up to."

She decided to tell him about Reece and the Hoffman farm in Reston. She briefly sketched in what had transpired on the visits she'd made there, but left out the fiasco involving the maniacal dog.

"She said she didn't call you?" Jackson's eyes met hers. A slight frown wrinkled his forehead.

"That's what she claimed." She held his gaze, as if the answer might be written in his hazel eyes.

"But you don't believe her. Could it have been someone else? Someone who sounded like her?"

"It's not that I don't believe her. It's just that—well, there was something in her eyes that wasn't right, like maybe she was afraid or something. And I know she hasn't been in touch with that New York agency where she works. That doesn't seem normal to me."

"Have you tried calling that number you think was hers?"

"Several times," Liz said. "No one ever answers. But it's not just the phone thing. The grandmother that Reece said she'd come to visit isn't around. She's Amish and seems to be out of town taking care of a relative. She left this cousin, Benedikt, in charge." She shrugged. "He's polite enough, but something doesn't sit quite right with me. And the housekeeper is something right out of Daphne du Maurier's *Rebecca*. Even Sadie says the place gives her the creeps."

Their food arrived, and they tucked in.

"They've got the place locked up like Fort Knox," Liz continued. She described the premises, gesturing with her fork, but omitting the fact that she and Sadie had snooped where they didn't belong. "I know. I'm probably reading something that isn't there, and Ben did say Reece gets confused when her migraines act up. I think I'd feel better if I talked to the grandmother."

Jackson looked across at her, his mouth set, eyes gentle but unreadable. "Would it help if we took a ride into Reston? I know a shop owner who deals with Cross Furniture from time to time. She might know something."

Liz leaned forward. "That would help. When did you have in mind?" she asked, excitement building.

"How about now?" he suggested.

"Can you? I mean, don't you have work to do? Meetings?"

"There is always work to be done. But this is important to you, so work can wait. Let's see if we can put your mind to rest once and for all about Hoffman and Mrs. Danvers." He smiled at his literary reference and reached across to grasp her hands. "Don't you worry, Liz. We'll get to the bottom of this."

———————— *//////////////////////////* ————————

Forty-five minutes later, for the fourth time in a week, Liz arrived on the outskirts of Reston. The town was a good deal smaller than Pleasant Creek and lacked its unique charm. But streets and shops appeared to be in reasonable condition. The people they could see out and about seemed to be mostly farmers, women in casual attire, and young children not yet of school age. Several cars were parked along the curb, and near the feed store a horse stamped in front of a parked Amish buggy.

They passed the courthouse, a yellow brick building with a clock at the top of its short spire. A row of yew bushes languished beside the steps, along with not-yet-blossoming daylilies that were in need of a good pruning.

"Do you know any of the city management?" Liz asked.

"The former sheriff," he said. "Ron Haggedorn, but everyone calls him 'Hack.' He had to give up the job after an illness. Good man and an excellent lawman, but he's not taking his forced retirement too well. The new guy's name is Rex Bladen. I hear he's kind of a ramrod. I haven't had any contact with him."

Jackson passed through the main section of the town, drove a mile or two beyond, and pulled up to a midsize building with a sign that read *Devon's Home Accents.* The glass-fronted structure was well-lit and displayed some small furniture pieces, along with home decor like table lamps, colorful vases, and framed pictures. "We supply this place with small tables and bedside pieces every so often. They don't have a lot of space, but the shop owner likes our work and directs visitors to Cross Furniture for larger items," Jackson explained.

Liz got out of the car and followed Jackson inside. Maybe the proprietor was acquainted with Mrs. Hoffman and could help locate her. Better wisdom told her she shouldn't pry. Why was she borrowing trouble?

"Jackson! What a pleasure to see you." The woman came around the service desk. She was somewhere in her late fifties or early sixties and seemed far too sophisticated for the town of Reston. She wore her graying dark hair in a careless yet elegant knot at the nape of her neck. Wispy tendrils strayed onto the shoulders of her navy dress, which was set off by a red-and-white paisley scarf. The name tag affixed at the left lapel of her dress read *Anita Devon.* She turned inquiring brown eyes on Liz.

"Good to see you too," Jackson said. "This is Liz Eckardt. She owns the Olde Mansion Inn in Pleasant Creek."

Anita extended her hand. "I've heard good things about your inn." She frowned slightly, no doubt wondering why Liz would come to a store when she was obviously acquainted with the owner of Cross Furniture and could get whatever she needed right at home.

"Thank you," Liz said. "Your shop is lovely, Anita."

The woman smiled. "What can I do for you folks today? We have a spectacular spring sale going on right now."

"Actually, Liz and I stopped in because we were wondering if you might know an Amish lady with the last name Hoffman. We understand she owns a farm near here."

Bless him for easing her hesitation and broaching the subject for her. "Her first name is Lovina," Liz added.

"Yes," Anita said, brightening. "I know Lovina Hoffman. A fine woman. She doesn't come in often, but she's always so kind. A few years ago, my aunt had a stroke, and Mrs. Hoffman was very good to her, especially during the last few months of her life. I've always been grateful to her."

"Do you know where I can find her?" Liz asked. "You see, her granddaughter, Reece, and I met each other during a plane ride. I'd like to stop in and see Reece again, and I've heard she's in town visiting her grandmother." It bordered on a white lie, but Liz didn't know how to explain her interest any other way.

"Oh, sure. She has a farm not far from here." Anita frowned. "But I don't think she's there right now. She's staying over in Bradyville with an elderly woman who was my aunt Charlotte's neighbor. I think she's related to Mrs. Hoffman." She chuckled, making crinkly laugh lines around her twinkling eyes. "I have fond memories of her. She lives on Wesley Road where it intersects with Dunn. It's a white two-story with green shutters. There's a small red barn and a chicken coop on the property."

"Thank you," Liz said. "Maybe I'll pop over and visit with them."

"I'm sure they would enjoy that, dear. Now, Jackson, I'll need half a dozen more of those small round tables I ordered last month. I can't keep them in stock. You and your men do such excellent work. I'll call the order in, but I wanted you to have a heads-up. Oh, there's my next appointment. Feel free to poke around, and let me know if there's anything else I can do for you." She went to greet a customer who had just entered the shop.

Liz and Jackson browsed the shop's wares for a few minutes, then made their way back to the car.

"It's good to have someone with connections on my side," Liz told him, linking her arm through his. "Now I know where to find Reece's grandmother."

"Do you want to go see her now?" he asked, glancing at his watch.

"No, it's getting late," Liz said reluctantly. "I have to get back for coffee hour. Besides, I need to think about how to approach her and what to say that won't make me sound like I'm snooping into her affairs." Liz glanced up wryly at Jackson. "I know. That's what I'm doing, but only because I'm worried about Reece."

"Because you care," he said with a wink and pressed her arm against his side.

Liz's cell phone jangled. She reached into her pocket. "Hello, Sadie," she said as she answered it.

"You home?" Sadie asked.

"No, but I will be within an hour or so." Liz heard an anxious note in her friend's voice.

"Then I'll wait for you. I need you to take me to the police station. They found my Jeep."

Sadie clicked off before Liz could say anything more. Liz frowned at the phone. If Sadie's beloved Jeep had been recovered, why didn't she sound happier about it?

10

Sarah was arranging pastel napkins for coffee hour when Liz arrived back at the Olde Mansion Inn. There had been no sign of Penny when she'd picked up her car at the courthouse. The white BMW should have been in the parking lot—unless Penny had decided to take a coffee break and have refreshments at the inn.

But there was no sign of her there either.

"Sorry I left you to get things going by yourself," Liz told Sarah as she tied her apron around her waist, shoving Penny from her mind. "Lunch took a little longer than I planned."

Sarah gave her a shy smile. "Did you and Jackson have a nice time?"

"We did. We decided to take a little drive over to Reston after we left The Coffee Cup."

"Isn't that where you went to return the suitcase to the woman you met on the plane?"

"That's right."

Liz arranged cucumber-and-cream cheese sandwiches on a glass plate while Sarah set out the fresh blueberry-apricot puffs that Liz had baked before leaving that morning. The coffee was brewing, the hot water for tea was ready, and guests would arrive any moment. What to do about Reece Hoffman and the grandmother in Bradyville would have to wait.

June Anderson entered the sitting room and sat down in one of the soft armchairs near the fireplace, which wasn't lit on this warm spring afternoon. Liz wondered where June's husband was. From the tense expression on his wife's face, Liz thought it was a safe guess that Karl was no less preoccupied with whatever was worrying him than he had been that morning and the day before.

"Good afternoon, June," Liz greeted her. "May I pour you some of this new tea blend I found? It has spice, cocoa, and caramel flavors. We also have a nice green tea and a cinnamon herbal. Of course, there's coffee as well—dark roast, hazelnut, or regular."

"I'll try that energizing variety. Karl and I walked our feet off downtown. Perhaps I can bring him a cup. He's resting right now."

"Any word on your stolen merchandise?" Liz asked, handing June her tea.

She shook her head. "Not yet. It may take some time, the authorities say."

"Of course that's what they say," said Vera in her severe way, coming in and sitting down on the adjacent sofa. "Everyone knows how exceedingly slow the wheels of justice grind, or whatever the saying is. Could I have a cup of plain, black coffee?"

Ever the voice of cheer. But Liz knew Vera's bark was worse than her bite. She smiled at Vera. "Of course. Where's Violet?"

"Probably mooning over that man she's been stepping out with." She twitched her nose and took a sip of her coffee. "She couldn't even stitch a decent Shoofly quilt block today. Just kept peering off into space like a silly schoolgirl."

Stepping out. A quaint, old-fashioned phrase, so Vera-like. Liz smiled to herself. Indeed, Violet had seemed preoccupied the last couple of days. And Liz had seen her and Stefan several times at the gazebo. "Well, I think it's wonderful that your sister is enjoying the company of a fine man like Stefan," she said. "Won't you try a sandwich? They're light and refreshing."

Vera declined the offering and turned to talk to June about the latest fabrics available in Sew Welcome. Liz went into the kitchen to replenish the sweets tray and was surprised to see Violet sitting at the table by herself. Her usually smiling face was wreathed in worry, her merry eyes filled with tears, and she twisted a lace-edged handkerchief in her hands.

"Violet!" Liz exclaimed, taking the chair next to the older woman. "What's happened?" She pulled her chair closer and put an arm around Violet's shoulders.

"Oh, Liz," Violet wailed. "I don't know what to do. Stefan has asked me to—" She choked back a sob. "He wants me to marry him."

"Then why are you upset, Violet? I thought you were head over heels for Stefan. You said you two have been corresponding all year. I thought he might propose, and I thought you would accept."

"Vera would never—I couldn't—oh, what am I going to do?"

"Surely your sister would want you to be happy," Liz said, realizing that Vera was the cause of Violet's hesitation. As far as Liz knew, the two sisters did everything together. They had taught for years in the same school, retired the same year, and lived together. "Vera wouldn't stand in the way of your happiness." *Or would she?*

"Stefan wants us to live here in his house." She brightened a bit. "It needs a woman's hand, but it's a delightful little cottage with lots of room for a garden, and I love it here in Pleasant Creek. Oh, Liz! What am I going to do?"

"You'll still be within a few hours of your sister, and she can come and visit you here. She loves Pleasant Creek too," Liz said soothingly. "She'll get used to the idea."

"Do you really think so?" Violet asked.

"I do. You must decide what you truly want and what is right for you. Then be strong enough to go for it." Liz held Violet's watery gaze. To marry at seventy-plus must be a difficult decision, but then who could put an age limit on happiness? And sweet Violet so deserved to be happy. Desperate to see the older woman less miserable over something she wanted, Liz said, "Do you want me to talk to your sister?"

"Would you?" Violet's round face beamed through her tears. "I know she's obstinate and prickly as an old porcupine, but she likes you. She trusts you."

"Of course I'll speak to her, but in the end, you'll have to choose no matter what your sister says." Liz pulled a clean dishcloth from the drawer, dampened it with cool water, and gave it to Violet. "Now we don't want to waste those pastries out there. I made them fresh this morning."

Sarah came into the kitchen with the teapot as Liz was giving Violet a parting hug. Liz winked at her over Violet's shoulder to signal all was well, though she was already wondering what she had been thinking in offering to approach the formidable Vera about such a big change. Vera—who groused over the amount of time Violet spent on the phone with Stefan and the "late" hours she kept when visiting with him—surely would not jump at the idea of Violet marrying him and moving hours away from her sister.

As Violet went out into the sitting room, Liz heard Sadie's voice from the rotunda and remembered her promise to accompany her friend to the police station to retrieve her car. The day was turning out to be a full and challenging one. "Can you finish up, Sarah?" Liz asked. "Sadie's Jeep has been found, and I'm going to take her to pick it up."

"That is delightful news. Don't worry about anything." Sarah pushed up the sleeves of her dress as she prepared to attack the dishes in the sink. "I'm so glad she's getting her car back." She smiled at Liz. "Mary Anne says Sadie's been like a bear with a lost cub."

"I know. I shouldn't be long."

Then again, when does anything go the way it should?

———— //////////////////////// ————

"We lifted some prints from your car, Sadie, but so far no matches to anyone in the local and national databases have shown up." Chief Stan Houghton sat across from Sadie and Liz in his office. Fiftyish and graying, the chief was well-respected in the community and known both for his shrewd peacekeeping and his ability to get along with the sometimes-uncooperative Amish, who usually chose to handle difficulties within their own communities under the direction of their bishop. Calling for aid from the local police was reserved only for the direst circumstances.

Liz was fond of the chief, who—despite working with lawbreakers—remained warmhearted and genial. They had worked together on other mysteries, which she seemed to attract like a magnet, and her appreciation for him had developed into a trusting friendship.

"I'll need a statement from you once you've examined it," the chief told Sadie, interrupting Liz's reverie. "Include anything missing inside and any damage that wasn't there before your car was taken."

"Where did you find it?" Liz asked.

"A landfill several miles from here."

Sadie shot forward in her chair. "A dump? They left my beautiful Jeep in a dump?"

"And well-hidden at that. We found it at the far end where the forest begins. It was behind a maze of overgrown trees and a mound of junk six feet high." The chief narrowed his gaze. "They've got to do better about managing that place. I cited them." He tucked his phone into his shirt pocket and pushed back from the desk. "Well, if you're ready, let's go out back so you can claim your property. We did run her through the car wash for you. She was pretty muddy."

Sadie got to her feet. "No hits on the prints, so no record, huh? Those skunks," she grumbled under her breath. "Gunning my poor Jeep across the countryside and leaving her in a dump! They deserve to be in jail, not out there ripping off someone else's wheels."

"When we find them, we'll prosecute," Houghton said grimly as he led the way out of the station and toward the back lot. "And we will find them."

"When I find them, I'll tan their hides!" Sadie said. Liz was sure she would, unless the chief managed to stop her. She hurried to catch up with Sadie's determined strides.

The Jeep seemed no worse for wear, its pink exterior gleaming from being newly washed. Sadie walked around the vehicle, checking for damage. She noted a few minor scratches, but overall, she declared her baby's exterior sound.

She unlocked it and peered inside. The old quilt that she always kept in the car lay askew on the back seat. "Well, they didn't want my quilt," she said with an ironic smile. "That old rag keeps me warm on cold mornings before the heat kicks in."

But the Jeep's interior had been ravaged. The glove compartment hung open and its contents—papers, tissues, gloves, a bag of peanuts—were scattered on the floor. There were, however, no slashes or rips in the upholstery. "Well, that's a relief. Good thing I don't store anything valuable in the glove compartment. But I have a lockbox bolted onto the back seat, since there's no trunk to speak of," Sadie explained as she walked around to the rear of the vehicle. "I had it made special. It's where I put stuff so it's not visible to the passersby."

"Clever," Liz said.

"It's completely invisible when the back seat is down." Sadie opened the rear door. She reached inside and flipped a small trigger on the left side. The seat flipped up, revealing the box. "No!"

The box was open, and all around its frame were gouges and scars likely made by a crowbar or some other tool. "Did you have anything inside that box?" Chief Houghton asked.

"Just the stuff I bought at the flea market," Sadie said, frowning at the damage to her back seat. "What in the world would kids want with old flea market junk?"

Chief Houghton was making notes on his phone. His thick eyebrows raised. "What were the items?"

Sadie stared at the empty box. "Two old brooches—just costume jewelry. One was a cat with green eyes. The other was a circular piece, gold-plated, pretty but worthless. Maybe those kids thought it was genuine. I only paid a couple dollars for it, so it definitely wasn't real."

The chief punched in some more notes. "Anything else?"

"An old painting—not huge—maybe ten by twelve inches or so, and nothing special. But it reminded me of one my grandmother had. I was afraid of it as a kid because it was so dark—a landscape with heavy clouds and gnarly trees that made me think of witches brooding over the land. I can't imagine what she saw in it, but she always kept it in the same place at the far end of the living room. Now it reminds me of her in a nice way. They wanted twenty bucks for it, but I got them down to ten."

"Okay," the chief said. "We'll keep an eye out." He replaced his phone in his pocket. "I'm glad you got your Jeep back."

Sadie got up and closed the hatch. "Me too—and if the scoundrels think they got anything more than a joyride, the joke is on them." She jingled her ring of keys in farewell. "I'll meet you back at the inn, Liz. Thanks for the ride."

Liz climbed back in her Acura and started the engine. It had been quite a day. Lunch with Jackson and learning the whereabouts of Lovina Hoffman. Then rushing back to the inn for coffee hour and trying to comfort a distraught Violet. The lives of her friends certainly were anything but dull. She smiled as she drove back toward the Olde Mansion Inn. Overall, it had been a good day. Sadie had her Jeep back, and Violet was hopeful that her sister would understand about Stefan.

She pictured Stefan—tall, burly from years of outdoor work, not an ounce of fat. He still had a full head of white hair and eyes the color of the sea when the sun shone on it. His wife had been gone for several years, and though he had loved her dearly, he had coped better than most men who had lost a spouse. But Liz had known how lonely he was and often saw him look out on the landscape with misty eyes. Now he had a chance for companionship, for new love. What could be better than that?

Yes, things were improving for her friends, but what about Reece Hoffman? Liz wanted to include her in that circle of friendship that made her life so fulfilling, but it seemed Reece had no such inclination. Why couldn't Liz just let it go? *When a person doesn't want your help or your friendship, you move on. Right?*

But that urgent phone call still nagged at the back of her mind. Had it been Reece? Was she being prevented from saying what she wanted to say? It had been four days since their meeting on the plane. What was happening to her? And why did it matter so much to Liz? After parking her car at the inn, Liz pulled out her cell phone and redialed the number of the mysterious caller. She'd tried it several times since that first call with only monotonous rings in response.

It only rang once. Liz's heart soared.

But it was voice mail—an automated response that sounded nothing like Reece. At least it was something. Liz left a message and clicked off.

As grateful as Liz was to be able to leave a message this time, she couldn't help but wonder why the change, and so soon after her latest visit to the farm. If only a real, live human would pick up, Liz might be able to set her mind to rest.

As it was, all she could do was worry about Reece.

11

The old-fashioned bell tinkled as Liz opened the door of Sweet Everything. It was early afternoon on Saturday, and the aroma of breads and pastries baked that morning still hung in the air. Naomi usually sold out quickly on weekends, but several customers lingered around showcases and sat at the small white tables with their colorful place mats.

Liz loved coming here and seeing what a success Naomi had made of the place. She was a natural in business, and her imaginative decorator cakes drew high praise. Liz smiled, remembering how she and Naomi had clicked right away when she'd moved to Pleasant Creek.

She really needed Naomi's advice, so as soon as she could break away from the Olde Mansion Inn, she had sought out her friend.

"You really hit the ground running after your week away, didn't you?" Naomi said when they had cleared a spot in the little office off the busy kitchen. She pushed back a lock of sable-brown hair that had strayed from her chignon. Cheeks still rosy from baking highlighted the golden brown of her eyes and perfectly shaped brows.

"This week has been a full one. So much has happened," Liz said. She gratefully accepted the cup of coffee Naomi handed her. "I loved that little homecoming party you and the Material Girls gave me, by the way. It made me feel very special."

"Sadie's idea," Naomi said. "But most of us agreed you were worth the trouble." She winked.

"Did you hear? She got her Jeep back," Liz said. "We picked it up at the police station yesterday."

"I heard. Caitlin saw her at the auto supply store buying one of those anti-theft locks that keeps the steering wheel from moving."

"Guess she's taking no chances on it being stolen again," Liz said.

Naomi flipped her apron over her head and tossed it on a chair. "Caitlyn also mentioned that Stefan has been seeing a lot of that guest of yours, Violet Holmes."

"News travels fast!" Liz said. "He's asked her to marry him, but she's worried that her sister won't approve. She was in tears over it yesterday."

"Vera probably won't approve. She doesn't approve of most things, from what I've seen of her. But that shouldn't stop Violet from pursuing her own happiness." Naomi crossed her arms. "Violet deserves a man who will be good to her, and Stefan is a perfect gentleman."

"That's what I told her. And I promised I would speak to Vera on her behalf." Liz blew out her breath. "What was I thinking? I hope Violet will say yes, despite any guff from her sister. Think of the party we could throw for her. She could have the ceremony at the church here in Pleasant Creek, and the Heirloom Room makes into a really beautiful honeymoon suite—" She stopped. "I'm getting ahead of myself, aren't I?"

"Just a bit," Naomi said with a chuckle. "But I will make one masterpiece of a cake for them if they decide to embark on a life of conjugal bliss." She peered at Liz. "I get the feeling that's not what's actually bothering you. What is it?"

Liz sighed. "It's that young woman I met on the plane. I'm worried about her. I need to speak to her grandmother, but I can't think of a plausible reason for seeking her out clear over in Bradyville. I only know where Mrs. Hoffman is because a friend of Jackson's knows her. I didn't get anywhere with Reece's cousin, who's taking care of the grandmother's farm while she's tending a sick relative. He didn't exactly put out the welcome mat for me."

Naomi raised her eyebrows. "Are you sure you should get involved? I mean, you only met this girl once, and she doesn't seem anxious to talk to you."

"But she might have tried." Liz told her about the phone call. "I just have this feeling that it was her. The grandmother will want to know why I'm seeking her out. I don't want to alarm her about Reece." She shrugged. "I'm not entirely sure there's anything to be alarmed about. But Reece apparently hasn't been in touch with the modeling agency she works for. That seems really odd."

Naomi sipped her coffee, pondering Liz's concern. Then she brightened. "You know," she said thoughtfully, "Bradyville has an open-air market on Saturdays. Vendors sell fresh produce, herbs, and flowers for planting season, as well as a variety of pastries and crafts. We could just stop by the place where your Mrs. Hoffman is staying—since we were in the area anyway." A smile played about Naomi's lips.

"I could say I met her granddaughter traveling and was taking a chance that Reece might be there, since she told me her grandmother was her reason for coming to Indiana." She stopped, looked at her friend curiously. "Did you say 'we'?"

Naomi laughed. "Sure. I'm game for a little ride. Jenny can hold the fort here for a while. Besides, there won't be many more customers this late in the day. People know we sell out early on Saturdays, so they tend to come in the morning."

"It will probably be nearly four when we get there and vendors will likely be getting ready to close, but I'm willing to go if you are. Besides, the market's only an excuse anyway. Naomi, you're a genius. I knew you would think of something."

"Well, let's quit jabbering and get moving." Naomi grabbed a light jacket from a nearby hook. "You see if Sarah can manage coffee hour, and I'll touch base with Jenny then meet you outside."

When they reached Bradyville, many of the vendors were indeed packing up their supplies in the town square. A few, holding out for last-minute sales, remained at their posts. Liz bought a few herbs in small black pots and the last two loaves of specialty bread. Naomi bought an azalea plant and a bouquet of merry daffodils tied with a raffia ribbon.

After depositing their purchases in the trunk of Liz's car, they headed north on Wesley Road, scanning signs carefully for Dunn Road. Just past the junction, Liz saw a white two-story house perched on a hill and beyond it a small red barn. "And there's the chicken coop Anita mentioned," she said, pointing.

Liz was struck by the immense contrast between this pleasant place and the gloom of the Hoffman farm. The buildings on this small farm were weathered but well-constructed, and the grounds were neat. In the field, surrounded by a log fence, two cows and a horse grazed. As they drew closer, Liz spotted an Amish buggy parked near the barn. They drove up the short driveway and parked the car near the buggy. Chickens pecked the dusty ground, clucking furtively as they strutted in search of grain. An old black-and-white dog greeted them without barking and held his tail erect in a wary pose.

"Hey, fella," Naomi crooned softly, holding her hand out, palm up.

Liz, holding the box of apple muffins Naomi had packed, said, "What a good dog," and the animal's tail began to wag. She and Naomi walked to the house with the dog frolicking alongside, as carefree as if they were old friends. Seeing no bell, Liz rapped on the door and sent up a short prayer.

The door opened to reveal a woman dressed in traditional Amish garb. She was matronly, not more than five feet tall, and had the sleeves of her plain blue dress rolled up to her elbows. The strings of her black Kapp hung down over her snowy-white apron. Tendrils of curly gray hair strayed damply around a face rosy with exertion. Her eyes were a deep shade of blue that seemed lit from within.

The woman frowned slightly and wiped one hand on her apron. "*Ja?* What is it?" Her tone was polite, the accent strong.

"Mrs. Hoffman?" Liz asked.

"Ja." She glanced from Liz to Naomi and back again, her brow wrinkled in confusion.

"My name is Liz Eckardt. I run a bed-and-breakfast in Pleasant Creek. This is my friend Naomi Mason. I'm sorry to bother you, but I was hoping—that is, my friend and I were shopping at the Bradyville market, and we thought we'd stop here before going home. Anita from Devon's Home Accents in Reston told us you were here taking care of someone who is ill."

Mrs. Hoffman seemed no less puzzled. She clasped both hands over her apron.

Liz hurried on, sorry to cause the concern she read in the woman's face. "I met your granddaughter, Reece, while traveling recently, and she told me she was coming to visit you. I was hoping that we might see her since we were passing through anyway."

"But she is not here," Mrs. Hoffman said. "You know my Reece? You have talked to her? I have not seen her in so long." She gestured inside. "Please, come in."

Lovina led them with quick steps into the living room. Shades were half-drawn against the late afternoon sunlight that speckled the plain walls. A quilt was folded on a wooden bench near the fireplace. The room also held two straight-backed chairs and a rocker, and on a small table were a kerosene lamp and a large Bible. Liz loved the simplicity and coziness of Amish homes and the fragrant aroma of baking that invariably clung to them. There was, however, a hushed atmosphere here. The stillness that came with sickness pervaded, and there were no children's voices. Mrs. Hoffman's relative must live in this house alone. It was unusual for the Amish elderly to be alone. They were almost always part of a large extended family that found room to care for them.

When they were seated, Lovina Hoffman leaned forward, her roughened hands twisting in her lap. Liz handed her the box of muffins. "We hope you'll enjoy these."

Lovina accepted the box and set it down on the immaculate table next to her. "Thank you." Her face registered excitement and then abashed curiosity. "Reece is coming to see me? But how do you know her?"

"I met Reece on the plane when I was returning from a conference in Maine," Liz explained. "She told me she was coming home to Indiana. To see you. She said you had been asking her to come back."

The blue eyes turned misty. "It has been so long," Lovina whispered. "My sweet Reece. After her parents—" She bit her lip as if to compose herself, then continued. "After her parents died, it wasn't long before she went away. I tried to keep in touch with letters. Many letters, and many were returned. She moved around so much, but I always hoped and prayed she would come back." She looked away to some memory—perhaps to a little girl sitting on her lap as she stitched a quilt. "It was so hard on her, my Reece." She straightened suddenly. "But forgive me, please. I have not offered you refreshments."

"No, please, there's no need," Liz said in quick response.

"I have coffee. Ja, I will get coffee." She rose, taking the box of muffins with her, and went into the kitchen, returning moments later with a tray—coffee and some small tarts and Naomi's treats on a plain white plate. She urged them to partake, and Liz and Naomi obliged. Amish baking was always a treat. Lovina sipped coffee in the silence that lay heavy in the room. When a low moan emanated from somewhere in the house, Lovina stood quickly. "Excuse me. I must see to Huldah." She flashed an imploring look at Liz. "Please don't leave. I will be right back. Then you must tell me about Reece."

Liz and Naomi drank the coffee and enjoyed the tarts until Lovina returned a few minutes later, carrying a towel and an empty glass. "My dear aunt Huldah," she explained. "She suffers so. She has little time left and did not want to leave her farm. The chickens, you know. They are special to her, so I take care of them—and her." She set the items on a table just inside the living room entrance. The wrinkles in her forehead deepened. "Please, where was my granddaughter going when you spoke to her on the airplane?"

"To your farm," Liz explained. "When we landed, we got our suitcases mixed up. I got hers and she got mine." Liz told her how she had discovered the error and had gone to the farm to make the exchange, where she had met Reece's cousin.

"Benedikt. He is helping at the farm while I tend to Huldah." Her voice was flat, unreadable. She frowned, as though trying to put all the strange bits of information she was hearing together. "He is very capable," she added and looked down at her hands.

Liz couldn't help wondering if Lovina was entirely comfortable with her "capable" grandson. There was no spark of pride or confidence, or perhaps she was simply preoccupied with thoughts of Reece and the sick woman in the room beyond.

Lovina's eyes met Liz's again, pleadingly. "When was it, Miss Eckardt? When did you meet my Reece on the airplane?"

"Monday, and please call me Liz," Liz said, not missing the calculation she read in Lovina's expression. Today was Saturday. Nearly a week, and Reece had not visited her grandmother.

"She was recovering from a migraine that night," Liz replied hastily. "So I didn't get to see her, but when I returned a couple of days ago . . ."

She hesitated, framing her words carefully. "I saw her then. She seemed much better, and Ben said she would visit you soon, right here in Bradyville."

Lovina was quiet a few moments as she processed this information from a stranger. Then she spoke. "I am grateful to you for coming to me. I am glad you met my Reece." She paused. "So long I have prayed, and now I will see her. Gött never fails us." She didn't ask further questions, such as what Reece might have shared with Liz of her life since leaving Pleasant Creek. Liz guessed this would be painful, and she felt a great sympathy for her. Lovina had already opened up to an Englisher she didn't know. It was a departure for the Amish, who usually kept their tight-knit secrets from outsiders.

Liz got up, as did Naomi. "I'm glad to have met her too. She is a lovely girl. I hope she—" Hoped what? That Reece really was all right? That she would not keep this faithful and loving grandmother waiting, but would get into her rental car and drive to Bradyville?

"I am glad she is at the farm. Gött will take care of her," Lovina said absently, then walked them to the door and opened it for them. "Thank you again."

Once inside the car, Liz started the engine but didn't put it in gear right away. She stared idly out at the landscape and the road below, where a vehicle suddenly sprang to life and roared away.

She sat, reflecting on everything she had heard from Lovina and wishing Reece had graced her with a visit sooner. She hoped that the girl would provide some happiness for the grandmother who clearly loved her. She sighed and turned to Naomi. "What do you make of that?"

"Mrs. Hoffman is a very nice woman—and so devoted to caring for her sick aunt. I'm sorry that her life has been so hard."

"Me too. She's lost so much family." Liz drove away from the farm, troubled but glad she had taken the time to find Lovina, to let her know of her granddaughter's intent to visit her. Surely the girl would come soon.

They headed back toward Pleasant Creek. Liz made a conscious decision not to dwell on the problems of other families—problems she couldn't solve, however much she wanted to. Love demanded a high price. It was those nearest and dearest who stepped so heavily on the heart. Her mind raced to faraway Kosovo where her godson, Steve, was serving in the military. She'd raised him as her own after his parents had been killed when he was in elementary school. How would she feel if she learned he had returned to America but hadn't contacted her? She felt an even stronger stab of sympathy for Lovina.

"Isn't that the same car we saw before?" Naomi squinted into the side mirror, then twisted around in her seat.

"What?" Liz came back to the present at the sound of Naomi's voice.

"The car that was at the bottom of the hill when we left the house. He's behind us now."

Liz checked the rearview mirror. "Probably lots of black cars behind us," she said. "Some have passed us too. This county road is the only connection between Bradyville and the highway, isn't it?"

"Yes, but that one has stayed behind us for the last two miles or more."

Liz shrugged, but she slowed down considerably, giving the driver behind an opportunity to pass. But the distance between them remained the same.

"I think he's following us," Naomi said.

Liz pressed the accelerator. The black car sped up as well. Who would be following them? Besides, it was still light, and the road, though not heavily traveled, was far from isolated. Still, Liz felt unnerved. Were they both imagining things? Had they been involved in too many mysteries and now imagined skulduggery where there was none?

Liz turned toward Pleasant Creek, tensing as she checked the rearview mirror again. The black car turned too—but in the opposite direction. Surprised at her giddy sense of relief, she said, "See, he wasn't following us."

Naomi said nothing.

Liz took a deep breath, determined to relax, but something in the back of her mind whispered, *What if I'm wrong?*

12

After dropping Naomi off, Liz headed home, eager for a quiet evening. Jackson had gone to Chicago for work and wouldn't get back until late. He'd call as he usually did to let her know when he was safe at home, but she was glad for some time to herself. She felt as if she had been on a conveyor belt all week and needed to unwind and catch up.

Saturday night in Pleasant Creek was generally quiet, though the playhouse was currently offering a semiprofessional run of *A Midsummer Night's Dream*. She had made sure there were flyers at the inn detailing showtimes alongside the brochures of restaurants and other attractions in the area that she usually kept for her guests.

The Andersons were planning to take in the play, for this was the actual date of their anniversary. That morning, Karl had wanted to know where he might order roses for his wife, and Liz directed him to Heaven-Scent Flowers, the new florist shop in town. She was glad to see he'd come out of his worried stupor and remembered his anniversary. Violet was probably out with Stefan. Liz imagined they would probably also attend the play. Vera would likely spend the evening in her room with a pot of herbal tea and her current quilt project, as she was wont to do. It was anyone's guess what Penny would get up to. Liz hoped she would make herself scarce, which seemed likely given her habits thus far.

As she entered the inn she noticed that the door to Sew Welcome was still open. She remembered that Sadie had planned to stay late. The town market was only days away, and Sadie had "a million things to do" for the special event that could bring in extra income for the shop.

Liz stepped through the doorway of Sew Welcome just in time to see Sadie brush her hair back from her forehead with her fingers after stacking some fabric on a shelf. It always amazed Liz how Sadie kept up her hectic pace. Widowed and living alone, she still ran circles around the younger Material Girls.

Liz heard a voice that wasn't Sadie's. Violet stepped out from behind a tall fixture, carrying another bolt of fabric. Dressed in purple slacks and a ruffled white blouse, she was obviously helping, chattering happily as she worked. A bracelet of purple beads that matched her necklace rattled on her chubby wrist.

"I saw her last night when Stefan brought me home," Violet said, making sure the bolt of polished paisley cotton was level with the one she had just placed. "I could hardly believe it was her."

Liz walked toward them, feigning nonchalance. She stooped to pick up a packet of buttons that had slipped to the floor.

"It was a bit late," Violet continued. She lowered her eyes as though she had breached a curfew and giggled. "Can you believe Miss Stryker was wearing jeans and a black leather jacket? And all that beautiful hair was stuffed up into a baseball cap. And I think I saw a strange man getting out of her BMW."

"Well, that's quite a change," Sadie said. "Miss Fancy Fran is usually dressed to the nines and flaunting her designer suits and hats."

Liz had not seen Penny dressed down in the short time she'd known her. She was always sporting those four-inch heels that sent her towering over everyone. But why not be comfortable when you were away from the office? Liz loved wearing jeans and a floppy flannel shirt. A bit of gardening in old clothes and a walk with Beans around Jaynes Lake could be downright soothing after a long day. Where did Penny Stryker go after hours? Maybe to see a boyfriend or visit the aunt she had mentioned when they'd first met?

Mind your own business, she told herself and stepped up to the counter where the two were talking. "Well, aren't you two the busy bees."

"Liz!" Violet said with a wave and rattle of her purple beads.

"There's not much time left before the town market," Sadie said. "We gotta make hay while the sun shines. Violet has been keeping me company."

"I'm always happy to help, but I have to be going now." She put a hand to her gray curls, blushing. "Stefan and I have a date." She slipped past them and out of the shop, leaving a wisp of lilac fragrance behind her.

Liz pulled out a chair for Sadie and another for herself. "Don't you ever go home?" she asked with mock reproof. "You shouldn't work so hard, especially on a Saturday."

Sadie tugged at the hem of her sweater and rested her hands on her hips. "Well, you know what they say—at least what Mother Goose says: 'Saturday's child works hard for a living.'"

Liz laughed at the reference to the old poem and flopped into the chair, letting her purse drop to the floor. "And I was born on a Thursday," she replied, "which means I have far to go."

"You and Naomi went pretty far today," Sadie said with a shrewd twinkle in her blue eyes. "All the way to the Bradyville produce market. Did you learn anything?"

"We found her grandmother, but it was awkward. Reece hasn't contacted her yet, and I could hardly share my concern about her and her cousin, Ben. I really don't understand it. Reece told me that Lovina was the reason she was making this trip back to Reston."

"Well, she strikes me as a pretty self-absorbed young woman," Sadie said in her usual straightforward manner. "She didn't even bother to thank you for returning her suitcase, did she? At least, not until we showed up there the third time."

Liz shrugged. "She may have a reason we don't know about," she said softly. "I still think something isn't right at that farm. Maybe something Reece has no control over." She bent to help Sadie secure the lid on a large tub. "I'd like to get a closer look at that place. There sure doesn't seem to be much farming going on. I want to know what Ben is up to."

She also would like to know whether it had anything to do with the car she and Naomi had seen that afternoon—the one that had followed them from the farmhouse to the highway. If it *had* been following them. She shivered. Was she seeing trouble where there was none?

Sadie pushed the tub off to one side and sat down next to Liz. A frown perched between her white eyebrows like a cautious sparrow. She sighed in an unusual exhalation of weariness.

"I think Saturday's child may have been working too hard after all," Liz said, giving Sadie an affectionate smile.

"Nothing of the kind!" she said, crossing her arms over her light cardigan. "I've just been doing some thinking about *my* problem." She pursed her lips. "Which really isn't a problem at all. I've got my car back. No big deal, right?" She looked off into some space Liz couldn't see. "But I've been wondering about the stuff I bought that day."

"You think something you bought might have been valuable after all?" Liz asked.

Sadie shrugged. "I didn't think so at the time, but Chief Houghton keeps asking me all these questions. When I was giving him detailed descriptions of the items I bought, I remembered something that didn't occur to me before." She tapped a finger against her jaw. "There were several people around when I first saw that painting that reminded me of the one my grandmother had. When I stooped to pick it up to take a closer look, another hand was reaching for it."

"Whose?"

Sadie shrugged again. "A little skinny guy wearing one of those bucket hats, the kind you can buy for a few bucks at the flea market. I just held onto the painting—it reminded me of my grandmother, and I wasn't letting it go without a fight—and the guy backed off. When I looked up, he was gone."

Liz stiffened. "And you think maybe—" She broke off, considering this new information. "You think he was after the painting too?"

Sadie's eyebrows rose. "Well, if he was after it or that costume jewelry I bought, he didn't fight me for it at the time. Didn't say a word or ask if I was going to buy it. He just took off. I figured it was an idle interest, and he wasn't going to push the matter. But what if he was watching? I mean, suppose he really wanted it and watched me put it into the Jeep?"

"And when you went across the street to the fruit stand, he saw his chance." Liz stopped, thinking the scenario through. "Maybe he didn't see anything inside and realized he'd have to take the whole car or risk you coming back and stopping him." She remembered the jimmied lockbox and the scars around it, proving someone had forced it open. "Then when he had what he wanted, he junked the car." Liz stared hard at Sadie. "That's pretty bizarre."

"Stan asked a lot of questions about the painting. He made me describe it in as much detail as I could." Sadie got up and moved to the desk she kept at the front of the shop. She came back with a handful of papers and shucked a few off the top. "He asked me to go through these. They're catalog pictures of valuable art and antiques that have been stolen in several recent burglaries."

Liz perused three pages of expensive items that had disappeared from several shops, including Karl and June's shop, The Golden Leopard. The items had been enlarged and printed in color, each item affixed with a price. It was a dazzling array worth a fortune.

"Nothing I picked up resembles any of the jewelry pieces," Sadie said firmly. "Not by a long shot." She turned over the page to reveal a gilt-framed landscape painted in dark blues and greens. Naked trees stood out against the heavily clouded sky, their branches crooked and knobby, like ancient blackened bones appealing to the heavens.

Liz felt a chill spreading through her own bones as she read the description, "'Eighteenth-century Chesley Austin landscape, valued at $250,000, stolen from The Golden Leopard in Chicago.'" She turned to a very quiet Sadie, who was staring at the picture with bemused consternation.

"It's a lot like the one I remember, but of course, it isn't the same one." Sadie's voice grew nostalgic. "I'm sure my grandmother's picture wasn't authentic at all. An excellent copy perhaps, but when her house burned, everything went with it."

Liz studied the picture. "I'm not a collector and don't know much about the art world. I've never owned an original painting except the ones Steve did in grade school. But wouldn't it be crazy if that painting you bought for a pittance was the real thing?"

"It's simply not possible that an expensive original would wind up in a flea market displayed with all the junk that ends up there." Sadie turned wide eyes to Liz. "Is it?"

"I can't imagine how, but if some mistake was made, if somehow it did wind up there . . ." Liz tried to imagine how it could happen. Could the person who stole Sadie's Jeep have known about the missing art and tracked it to the flea market? But how could anyone do that?

Sadie drew a deep breath and let it out in a weary stream. "Well, it's too bad for whoever owned it. Stolen once and stolen twice, if the painting I bought was authentic. I'm glad it's gone. I wouldn't want a valuable thing like that in my house, especially if other people were after it. And can you imagine if the police traced it there and I had to explain how I wound up with art worth a quarter of a million dollars? Even though I've told him my flea market painting was stolen, I'm sure Stan would have more than a few questions."

"Then I'm glad it's missing too," Liz said, handing the sheaf of papers back to Sadie.

"I didn't get a good look at the guy who was reaching for it at the same time I was, but I told the chief what I could remember." Sadie frowned. "It was dark and dingy in there. Why would he wear sunglasses unless he didn't want to be identified?"

"You didn't see his face?"

Sadie shook her head. "I couldn't tell you what color his hair was or anything else. He had no mustache or beard that I could see. I just glanced at him because I was focused on the painting. He just raced off after I carried my finds to the front counter." She sighed. "I guess the old brain isn't as sharp as it used to be."

"Nonsense," Liz said, laughing. "That sharp brain of yours has gotten us out of more than one scrape. Maybe the chief will have a book of mug shots to go through. If the man has a record, you may be able to recognize him. But you have your Jeep back, and you don't have to worry about the painting, valuable or not. Whoever swiped it is long gone. I just feel sorry for the Andersons and others who have worked hard for what they own, only to have it ripped off."

"Yes. I do too." Sadie pursed her lips in thought. "Unlike some wealthy people who think they're too good to mingle with ordinary folk, June Anderson seems to love coming into the shop. She's very friendly. And she's quite good with a needle."

"Yes, she is a good conversationalist. I'll bet she's great at cocktail parties." Liz picked up her purse and got to her feet. "I better get going. Beans has been waiting a long time for his walk."

The dog greeted her with a long stretch and shuffled to the door.

"I'm glad to see you too," she said, scratching behind his ears. "Let me grab my walking shoes, and you and I will take a turn around the lake before it gets completely dark."

Low charcoal-gray clouds mingled with the setting sun and cast a pinkish light on the quiet lake. Liz always loved this time of day, especially in spring when everything bloomed with an awakening vigor. Lush grasses abounded at the water's edge where the husky croaking of frogs blended with the music of cicadas and crickets. She smiled at the thought that she would be able to fall asleep to their lullaby for the next few months.

Liz led Beans past the gazebo toward the lake's wooded area, where a faint moon already shimmered through darkening leaves. Redbud and magnolia mingled with the green elms, maples, and firs. She breathed in the beauty and serenity that abounded and tried to imagine how hard it must have been for her mother to leave. Despite spending most of her life in Boston, Liz couldn't picture herself anywhere but Pleasant Creek now.

She wondered what was going through the mind of young Reece who had returned—however temporarily—to her roots in the Amish community. Ben clearly was not Amish, or was no longer Amish, but Lovina clung to the old ways she had embraced long ago. Ways that included prayer for a granddaughter who had thrown off the constraints of her youth. Ways that took her to the bedside of a relative who needed her care. Families were important, and especially so to the Amish. Liz's heart ached for the old woman who had lost a connection to her granddaughter and clearly wanted nothing more than to be reunited with her. It was sad when families were torn apart by disagreement, deep sorrow, or lost faith. But despite all, nature continued to lend its newborn seasons, its fresh beauty and bounty that inspired hope in the human heart.

"Nothing in Boston could equal this, could it, Beans?" she asked aloud and was suddenly startled by the sound of her own voice. She turned instinctively as though someone else might have spoken, but she saw only the familiar landscape. An owl swooped across the lake to a high branch on the other side. As they passed through the wooded area, she thought she heard a rustling in the trees, but no wind blew, and the water was still as glass.

"I'm getting paranoid, old boy," she said in a softer tone as Beans sniffed at a fallen log. Darkness was falling quickly now, and she tugged him away, eager to get back to the safety of the inn. There was no reason to think someone was following her. Not here and not on the road back from Bradyville. Yet she'd been subtly on edge for days, ever since her encounter with Reece on the plane. It was completely illogical. Why couldn't she let the whole matter of Reece Hoffman and her family go? What was this inner compulsion that continued to nag at her?

She heard another disturbance in the trees. Footsteps? The wind picking up? Or something else? The instinct to run was strong, but she forced herself to walk steadily away from the woods and toward the open area.

There was the gazebo, surrounded by low bushes, the pale moon shining over it. She rounded the bend and made it to the inn where the automatic lights beamed, having clicked on at dusk.

Suddenly, Beans began to bark, straining at his leash in the direction they had just come from.

As this was extremely out of character for him, she glanced over her shoulder.

But all she saw were the dark, distant woods and the lake, lying serene and untroubled beneath a spring moon.

13

Monday morning dawned with a brilliant sun and the promise of a busy week. Sunday had passed in its usual quiet way—church, lunch with friends, and a much-needed nap in the afternoon. But it was not without some unsettled nerves over the theft of Sadie's Jeep and the uneasy stroll around Jaynes Lake with Beans. Her imagination, she admitted, could run away with her. But today she would be too busy to dwell on stolen antiques, mysterious calls, and night noises that meant nothing. Probably.

After breakfast there were errands to run, meals to prepare, and another meeting of the Material Girls in the afternoon. With the town market event only a few days away, time was of the essence.

When breakfast was over and the kitchen set to rights, Liz drove into town to run the errands she had put off in the press of things. As she approached the police station, she slowed down.

The chief was sure to be busy and probably didn't know anything further about the theft of Sadie's Jeep and its contents. And what could she say about her suspicions concerning Reece? No, she really shouldn't bother him.

But when she saw an empty spot along the curb close to the front door, she found herself pulling in. She put the Acura in park. *I'll just drop in for a minute.*

"Liz." The chief looked up from the papers on his desk. "What brings you to the halls of crime and punishment?" He gave her a crooked grin and sat back, gripping the arms of his chair, which he filled to near capacity. His shirt sleeves were rolled up, and his hair curled at his temples. When the chief was working a case—even from his office chair—he had the appearance of a man who'd been chopping wood for an hour.

"I was passing and thought I'd say hello, Stan," she said, pausing in the doorway. "If you're busy, just tell me to go away."

"I'm always busy, young lady," he said with mock gruffness, "but not too busy for you."

"Keep calling me 'young lady,' and I may never leave," she said, dropping down in a chair opposite him. She wasn't more than a dozen years his junior, which she supposed didn't make her exactly "young." She slung her purse over the back of her chair and took a deep breath. "I saw the catalog pictures you left with Sadie," she began. "It's pretty amazing to think she may have found a valuable painting at that flea market."

The chief stroked his jaw. "How it got there is a puzzle, to be sure," he said thoughtfully. "From Sadie's description, and the picture, we're pretty sure it *is* a genuine Austin. And it's very possible that the man hanging around the flea market while Sadie was shopping traced it to Pleasant Creek. Luckily, he didn't put up a fight over it. Sadie could well have gotten hurt." He shook his head. "We'll have her go through some mug shots of known thieves and hope she recognizes someone."

Liz nodded and let her breath out in a sigh.

"Is that all you had on your mind?" the chief asked, raising an eyebrow.

Stan was a very perceptive man, but it surprised her that he had tuned in to her mood so quickly. Their friendship had begun with the first mystery to fall into Liz's lap not all that long after she arrived in town. Since then, their respect for each other had grown, though he frequently discouraged her from getting into potentially dangerous situations, and she frequently did so anyway.

"Is everything all right?" he asked patiently.

"Yes," she answered, but she could hear the hesitance in her own voice. She considered how to phrase her concern about the Hoffmans.

"Would this have anything to do with that young woman over in Reston?"

"You've been talking to Jackson," Liz said, glad she wouldn't have to start her story at ground zero and grateful that Jackson had voiced her concern to the chief.

"He told me you think she might be in trouble and that you were trying to locate her family."

"I did meet her grandmother," Liz said slowly. "She's taking care of a relative in Bradyville. She hasn't seen her granddaughter and didn't know she had come to Reston. But Reece told me the whole reason for making the trip from New York was to see her."

"Maybe she just hasn't gotten around to it yet. It's only been a few days since you saw her feeling well enough to be out of bed. Maybe there were other things she wanted to do or people she wanted to see first. Or maybe she hasn't felt up to a long drive yet. She might also have gone over yesterday. Who knows?" The Chief spread his fingers. "You may be reading too much into this."

"Maybe," she conceded. "But there was that urgent nighttime call. It sounded like her."

"The cousin told you she can get confused when she has her migraines. Maybe she woke up, forgot where she was, and panicked."

"I guess." She drew a breath. "But I don't trust that cousin who's taking care of the farm while Lovina Hoffman is away. I think something funny is going on there. It's obvious they don't want anyone coming around." She thought about relating the escapade with the dog, but the chief was sure to bawl her out for trespassing. "Do you know the sheriff in Reston? I mean well enough to ask what he knows about Benedikt Hoffman?" She gave him her best pleading look.

"The sheriff in Reston is new to the area. Name's Rex Bladen. He's a transplant from Hooper County and rules with a strong hand from what I hear. He's the new kid on the block, trying to establish himself, and he doesn't welcome the interference of outsiders."

Liz waited while the chief clicked the end of the pen in his thick fingers—something he sometimes did when he was thinking.

He frowned and continued, "I stopped by to welcome him. Figured I should, though he's been in place almost two months. And I offered the assistance of Pleasant Creek's department should he ever need it." He seemed to ponder his next thought, and Liz sat forward in her chair. "I'm afraid he was offended by my offer, as though I didn't think he could handle things on his own."

Liz sat back with a sigh. "I see."

"But I did run a check on Hoffman," he added, raising an eyebrow. "There's nothing on him in the books." He gave her a sidelong look. "You're not going to get in over your head on this one, are you?"

Liz shrugged but didn't meet the chief's eyes. She got up, slung her purse over her shoulder, and gave him a quick smile. "Thanks, Stan. I appreciate the time—and it's always good to see you."

She barely heard his goodbye. Her head whirled with thoughts and half-forged plans—perhaps it was time for another visit to Bradyville to see if Lovina had heard from Reece. Maybe she'd make a casual visit to the Reston farm or a chat with neighbors. Or she might even take a quick trip to meet Sheriff Bladen for herself.

Ten minutes later, Liz was driving through a fog of questions and thoughts. Benedikt—Ben—had no prior arrests or convictions. And of course, Lovina Hoffman's trust in him couldn't be denied, could it? She ought to feel relieved, and yet, as she found herself once again in the small community of Reston, she felt the weight of anxiety binding her to the ground like a tether.

The Reston sheriff's department was a low-slung brick building with small windows set inside dark frames. The green space around the property was meager, and its small parking lot was way overdue for repaving. She parked and went inside, curious to meet Sheriff Rex Bladen.

A tall man hovered with his back to the door over the desk of a middle-aged woman. He wore a canvas vest over a white shirt, boots, and tight black jeans, into which he had managed somehow to thrust his hands. He was saying something to the woman in a loud voice but immediately turned at the sound of the door opening.

Liz looked from the silver badge on his vest to thinning blond hair and deep-set gray eyes. *Midthirties, clean-shaven, and intense*, she thought, sizing him up. He pulled his hands from his pockets and placed them on narrow hips, a question in his eyes.

"I'd like to speak to Sheriff Bladen," she said pleasantly, slightly put off by the large rings on his pinky fingers.

He nodded. The furrow in his tanned forehead eased, and a thin smile appeared. "Yup." He took a few steps toward her but didn't extend a hand. "Something I can do for you?"

Liz looked uncomfortably to the dark-haired woman, who seemed relieved at the interruption, and back at Bladen. "I'm Liz Eckardt from Pleasant Creek. I wonder if I could have a few minutes of your time. Is there somewhere we could talk?"

He gestured to a door a few paces away that held a brass plaque upon which his name was inscribed. Liz followed him into the newly painted room, which held a desk with two plain chairs opposite. It was strangely bereft of decoration or personality, except for another long, narrow name plaque perched on the polished pine desk.

"Ms. Eckardt, did you say?" he asked in a curious baritone voice, gray eyes sharpening.

"Call me Liz. I'll get right to the point. I met a young woman on a recent flight who's from this area. She's been visiting relatives on the Hoffman farm."

His eyebrows rose.

"I know you're fairly new to Reston, but perhaps you know the Hoffmans?"

"Of course," he said, drawing his lips together in a studious expression. "Lovina Hoffman and her grandson. Fine folks. I've recently drafted Ben to serve on a development committee here. Good business skills. Town needs 'em." He idly twisted the ring on his left hand.

"The woman I met on the plane—Reece—she's his cousin." Liz drew a breath. "We got our suitcases mixed up, and I went to the farm to make the exchange." She struggled to explain her concern. "She told me she was coming to visit her grandmother, but I saw Lovina a few days ago and she didn't even know Reece was in town."

The gray eyes stared blankly into hers. He crossed his arms over his chest and leaned back in the desk chair. "And how exactly can I help you?" he asked.

"Well, I—" Liz gave her head a little shake. She wasn't explaining herself well. "I just wondered if everything is okay at Lovina's farm. It didn't seem—I mean—Reece might be in trouble. I think she called me on the phone and asked me to come."

The lips pursed once more, and he passed a hand over his jaw. "And did you go to see her?" he asked.

"Yes. She said she was okay, but she certainly didn't seem like it." She must sound like a terrible busybody, snooping into someone else's business. Why couldn't she convey the severity of her feelings about the situation?

Bladen suddenly stood and placed both hands on his desk. "Well, Ms. Eckardt, let me put your mind to rest. I'm aware that Ben has his cousin visiting from New York. Actually, I had some business with him just yesterday and went out to the farm. I can assure you everything is fine there, other than that Reece is recovering from a particularly severe migraine. Now, if there's nothing else?"

It was clearly a dismissal. She rose and adjusted the strap of her purse. She thanked him and drove back toward Pleasant Creek. The sheriff had vouched for the character of Ben Hoffman, and he had confirmed that he'd seen Reece as late as yesterday. She didn't have to like the new sheriff, but he must know his business. She could put her mind to rest, surely. Couldn't she?

When she drove into the inn's parking lot later, her mind far from settled, she was surprised to see Stefan pacing around the gazebo. Around and around the white-latticed structure he walked, his hands stuffed in the pockets of his trousers, white hair blowing in the wind. He looked intermittently at the ground and then up at the inn.

She parked her car and walked toward the gazebo to greet the handyman, who had retired from Cross Furniture where he had worked as a craftsman. He took on projects for friends and neighbors to supplement his retirement income and keep himself active. She remembered the winter he had met Violet, and how the two of them had clicked. Perhaps they were soon to meet again at the gazebo. But as she neared, she saw an expression of profound sadness on the man's face. "Stefan? How are you?"

"Afternoon, Miss Elizabeth," he responded, appearing to notice her only at that moment, so deep was his concentration. Though they had become good friends, Stefan always referred to her by the polite appellation. Ever the careful dresser, he wore a tan jacket over a neatly pressed plaid shirt. The creases in his pants walked a straight line above polished Oxfords.

"Do you and Violet have plans for this beautiful afternoon?"

He looked down before answering, the wrinkles in his forehead deepening. "We did," he said sadly. "But she sent word that she's changed her mind."

It occurred to Liz that she hadn't seen Violet that morning. "Oh, I'm sorry," Liz said. "Is she ill?"

Stefan worked his lips, the hurt in his eyes palpable. "I don't know, but she . . . her sister . . ." His left hand curled around a piece of note paper, which Liz saw was lavender. Part of a tiny purple flower was visible at the top. "I found this under a rock in the gazebo when I arrived." He broke off, his hand trembling a little.

Liz stared at Stefan's stricken face and felt completely tongue-tied. What could have happened? She recalled the afternoon Violet had told her with tears that Stefan had asked her to marry him. Had Vera put a wedge between them?

"I don't suppose I should wait any longer," Stefan said in a distracted manner. Hunching his shoulders, he began to move away. Then suddenly he gave Liz a pleading look. "Will you make sure she's all right—that she isn't sick or—or needing anything?"

"Of course, I will," she assured him. She grasped his right hand. "Now, don't you worry. Violet thinks the world of you. She may just need a little time."

He pulled away with a polite nod and disappeared behind the gazebo.

With a heavy heart, she made her way to Sew Welcome, where she knew the Material Girls would be waiting. As she crossed the rotunda to the shop, she saw someone coming out, carrying a shopping bag in one hand and in the other a purse and what appeared to be a portion of a quilt. *The lady herself*, Liz said under her breath.

"Hello," Liz said, smiling broadly into the prim face of Vera Holmes.

Her step was jaunty for a woman in her late seventies, and her bearing indicated that she was especially pleased with herself. She adjusted her fingers around the handle of the Sew Welcome bag and peered over her spectacles. "I just came from picking up what I needed for my project," she said, patting the gold-and-blue quilted piece draped over her arm.

"Why, that's beautiful," Liz said, her concern temporarily on hold. When it came to her passion for quilting, something of the tightly laced Vera unspooled. The opinionated teacher had taken a liking to Sadie too—perhaps finding in her something of a kindred spirit. They could both stare the needles off a porcupine. "What is that pattern called?" Liz asked, peering down at the fabric without touching it.

"I don't think it has an official name. It combines the Ohio Star and the Log Cabin patterns." Her tone softened. "My grandmother came from Ohio. She taught in a one-room log schoolhouse there. I was determined to become a teacher like her. This pattern makes me think of her."

"You are quite the quilter, Vera," Liz said, meaning it. "And your color combination is lovely."

"The borders will be squares set on point within squares," Vera said proudly.

"Come on into the sitting room," Liz said with sudden inspiration. "Have some coffee with me. Or tea if you prefer."

Soon they were seated across from each other with cups of Lady Grey tea. Vera eyed Beans warily, and he reciprocated by opening one eye briefly and dropping his big head down on his paws.

Vera waxed eloquent on her mother's and grandmother's teaching careers as well as her own in Louisville schools. Liz listened with genuine interest, especially as Vera added that her female ancestors had shared her passion for quilting, which made her feel closer to them when she did it. When Vera seemed to run out of things to say about a career in education, Liz finally broached the matter that was prominent in her mind. "Is Violet also working on a special quilting project?"

Vera pushed her chin out. "Well, she should be, but I couldn't get her to stir out of that bed this morning."

Liz leaned forward. "Is she not feeling well?"

"Oh, she's fine. She's just mooning over that German sailor."

"He's not German," Liz interrupted as quietly as her frustration would allow. "His ancestry's Danish, not that that matters, and he hasn't been to sea in decades. He is a fine gentleman. He's also an excellent craftsman, highly thought of in this community. And he's very fond of Violet."

"German. Danish. Whatever," Vera said, putting her cup down with finality on the china saucer. "I don't know where she gets these funny notions. She's been cooped up in that room for two days. Won't even get dressed. Just lies under that comforter with a cloth over her head."

How could Vera be so cavalier about her sister's feelings? Liz silently counted to ten. "Did she tell you that Stefan has asked her to marry him?"

"It's utter nonsense to consider such a foolish step at her age." Vera pushed back in her chair, causing Beans to wake with a snort. "It's time she got that silly notion out of her head."

"I don't think it's a silly notion," Liz said. "I think it's wonderful that she's found someone she enjoys being with, someone who makes her feel special."

Vera blinked. "She'd never be able to make a transition like that at this stage in her life. She'd be miserable. Besides, Violet needs stability and a steady hand." Vera shook her tight curls and began gathering up her things.

Liz rose, blocking Vera's path to the door. "I'm surprised that you would stand in the way of your sister's chance for happiness."

Vera jerked her head up, clearly dumbfounded by the rebuke. "I believe I know my sister better than you do, Miss Eckardt. I know what's best for her." She turned on her sensible heels. "And I do not have to stand here and be insulted."

"I mean no insult, Vera. I know you love your sister, and you have been together a long time. Naturally, it would be a big change for you if your sister accepts Stefan's proposal, but—"

"Good afternoon, Miss Eckardt," Vera said and pushed through the door.

Beans heaved himself to a sitting position and gave a muffled grunt—his commentary on the proceedings.

Liz turned to the dog, whose jowls seemed to droop with commiseration. "I thought that went rather . . . *not* well. Don't you? These days, it seems like all I can do is make things worse."

14

"These portable display cases Jackson made for us are absolutely perfect!" Caitlyn raved as Liz stepped inside the fabric shop. The youngest of the Material Girls stood amid fabrics, notions, and the flurry of female activity. Her blue-polished fingernails fluttered like azure butterflies.

"He's always looking out for us," Liz replied, brightening as always at the mention of Jackson.

"You mean he's looking out for *you*!" Caitlyn responded meaningfully. "Not that I'm complaining. He really came through on this project. What a guy!"

"That's our Jackson. Now fill those gorgeous display cases with these bundled fat quarters," Sadie commanded, handing Caitlyn a bright package of fabric squares tied with narrow ribbon. "And don't pack them in too tight."

From a few feet away, Naomi popped up from behind a counter. The bangles on her arm jingled as she held up a jumbo-size spool. "I'll put the heavy-duty spools of thread in these boxes. Opal's packing the smaller ones in the clear cases."

Liz sank onto a chair, glad for the easy familiarity of Sew Welcome and her friends, who always cheered her no matter what else was going on. Her errands so far that day could hardly be declared successful. She had forgotten half the items she'd gone to town for, interrupted two law officers' schedules, and had a despairing Stefan outside and a moping Violet upstairs. Added to that, she might just have jeopardized the friendship and possibly the returning patronage of Vera Holmes.

"Hard day at the inn?" a voice said at her elbow. Naomi had left the packing boxes and fabric bundles to join her. She pulled a chair up beside Liz and sat down.

Liz gave her friend a tired smile. "Does it show?"

"Afraid so," Naomi said, cocking her head to one side.

"Well, I seem to be batting zero today. I just got Vera royally mad at me. She thought I was insulting her, but I just wanted her to consider Violet's position."

"You mean about Stefan?" Naomi gave a sympathetic nod.

"Yes. Violet was to meet him at the gazebo today, but she stood him up. I'm sure it's because Vera doesn't approve."

Naomi nodded. "Poor Violet."

"Did you know she didn't get out of bed today? She didn't even come down to breakfast. I told Vera she was standing in the way of Violet's happiness," Liz said. "That's when she stalked off in a huff."

"Did she now!" Sadie had drawn up behind them, obviously tuning in to the conversation. She set a cardboard crate on the table with a louder thud than was strictly necessary. "Well, we will just have to see about that." She put both hands on her ample hips. "Vera's a good woman, but sometimes you have to lead the horse to water."

"This is a glum-looking group," Opal observed as she strode over to join them. She dropped some spools into the large front pocket of her apron. "Has someone died?"

"No," Liz said, moving over to make room for Opal. "We were just talking about the star-crossed lovers—Violet and Stefan."

"Oh," Opal breathed. "It would be a big change for the Holmes sisters if Violet marries. They've been together all their lives, and they always come to Pleasant Creek together." She looked directly at Sadie. "I believe you're the one who helped her become truly comfortable with her quilting. She thinks a lot of you."

"It's true," Liz said, holding Sadie in her gaze. "Vera wouldn't even register at the Olde Mansion Inn this time unless she was assured you were still in charge of Sew Welcome. You might just be the one she'd listen to," Liz said meaningfully.

Sadie made a gesture with her hand as though sweeping the matter aside. "Mary Ann!" she called at the top of her voice. "Where's that pie you promised us?"

"Mary Ann baked a strawberry-rhubarb pie for our coffee break," Caitlyn said. She glanced at her watch, sending her bracelets clanking. "Now might be a good time. I'll give her a hand."

Mary Ann came out of the workroom, a red scarf tied around her hair. "Give me a minute. I'll wash my hands and cut the pie," she called. "Can you clear that table and set up chairs for all of us? Caitlyn and I will serve."

"Of course," Liz said. "Come on girls." A few minutes after they'd followed Mary Ann's instructions and seated themselves, Mary Ann brought in the sliced pie on a tray with plates and flatware. Liz's mouth watered in anticipation. Mary Ann's pies were delectable, no matter the variety.

"We heard the chief is still investigating the theft of your Jeep, Sadie," Naomi said, detouring from the subject of Violet. "Is it true that the painting you bought at the flea market was valuable after all?"

Sadie nodded. "It sure looks like it. I had it in my possession for all of five minutes," she said with a sigh. "As they say, easy come, easy go."

"But not for the Andersons," Liz commented. "It was probably one of the most valuable items stolen from their shop in Chicago. The chief thinks the stash from several similar robberies may have ended up in this part of Indiana." She lowered her voice at the sound of someone in the foyer. "Sadie's find appears to have been a genuine Austin landscape worth a quarter million dollars."

The Material Girls were silent for a few seconds at the mention of the staggering sum. Liz turned her attention to a noise at the door, but whoever was in the foyer didn't enter.

"I couldn't believe my eyes when I saw it propped up on that easel," Sadie continued. "I thought I was back in my grandmother's dining room. I always reckoned it was the ugliest thing in her house. All those gnarly trees twisting and swirling against a threatening sky scared me to death. In fact, when I was a kid, I used to tiptoe past it, thinking something might jump out of one of the trees and grab me. But I still wanted it now, just to remember my grandmother."

"I know what you mean," Opal put in. "My uncle had a statue in his house that frightened me. I used to shut my eyes when I walked by it."

Laughter lightened the mood. Caitlyn came in from the kitchen with a tray bearing a coffeepot, a sugar bowl, a cream pitcher, and napkins.

"Any word from Lovina Hoffman or her granddaughter?" Naomi asked, pouring herself a cup of coffee.

"No," Liz replied with a sigh. She hadn't told Naomi about her scary walk with Beans on Saturday night after dropping her friend off at home. Had it only been two days since they had visited Lovina, then the sensation of being followed on the way back? "I'd like to visit Lovina again—maybe tomorrow—to see if she's heard from Reece."

Naomi's face blanched and she shivered. "Has anything else happened? I mean, you haven't seen that car again, have you?"

Naomi had phoned Liz first thing Sunday morning to make sure Liz was all right, and Liz had reassured her, still believing that no one had been following them. But then there had been that odd sense of someone in the woods later that night. She hadn't told anyone about that and had since tried to convince herself that it was her imagination working overtime. "Everything's been quiet, but I'm still worried about Reece. I hope she's at least contacted Lovina by now."

"I'll go with you tomorrow," Naomi said.

"You sure?"

"Absolutely. What are friends for?" Color had returned to her face, and now her eyes were large with interest.

Suddenly, the half-open door to Sew Welcome was pushed fully open, and Liz saw Penny Stryker in a form-fitting dress of royal blue. A wide blue hat sprouting an enormous orange poppy covered her platinum hair.

She hesitated on her matching blue stilettos and seemed to be searching for someone. When her eyes fell upon Liz she strode forward, an orange shoulder bag swinging at her side. "So, this is the Sew Welcome fabric shop. I haven't had a minute to come by, but now . . ." She paused for effect. "Well, you see, I need to pay a visit in my official capacity."

At the far end of the table, Sadie fixed Penny with her most intimidating glare.

Penny continued, largely addressing Liz. "I must be assured that any establishment servicing the public be properly licensed. Since you've been in business for several years, I'm sure all is in order, but just the same, I must see the proper documents."

Caitlyn set the serving tray on the table and stood motionless. The flatware on the tray clanked loudly in the charged atmosphere. No one said a word for what seemed endless seconds, everyone staring at the blue-and-orange vision poised near the table.

Liz gaped at Penny. They had already received their permit for the market event. So what was this nonsense about Sew Welcome's license to serve the public? The woman showed up at the oddest times. "I can assure you—" Liz began, but stopped when Sadie stood up.

"The proper documents," Sadie said, her voice controlled steel, "are easily visible just inside the entrance to this shop."

Mary Ann pasted on a pleasant smile and pointed to the door where Penny had entered. "You will see the license, along with capacity restrictions, clearly posted for anyone to see."

Penny swiveled her elegant head to the indicated wall and turned around again. "Well, as long as everything is legal."

She seemed temporarily at a loss, realizing that everyone was frowning in her direction. Then she seemed to rally. "I must compliment you on a charming and delightful little shop. I'm afraid I've been so busy with everything needing my attention at the town hall that I haven't had time to stop in before. But everything seems to be in order here, and I hope to be able to return and better acquaint myself with your lovely wares."

In truth, things were rather in a jumbled state because of their preparations for the special sale. Liz realized that Penny was trying to extricate herself from an awkward situation. "We're having coffee," she said. "Why don't you join us?"

Penny registered awkward surprise, but made no move to sit down. Mary Ann dished up a piece of the pie, which she had thoughtfully heated in the microwave for maximum flavor. The scent of warm strawberries filled the room.

Just as the oohs and aahs began, Beans waddled through the door and headed for the table. The dog made a soft huffing sound as he headed toward the fragrant pie and dropped into a sitting position right at Penny's feet.

Startled, she teetered on her delicate stiletto heels and fell against the table, knocking her purse to the floor and her enormous blue hat into the pie.

Shocked silence reigned.

Liz hurried to Penny's side. "Oh, I'm so terribly sorry! Are you all right?"

Penny's horrified shriek lanced through the air as everyone stared at the blue hat with its orange poppy completely engulfing their destroyed pie.

While Naomi lifted the hat from the mess with delicate fingers, Liz tried to steady a mortified Penny and straighten the bodice of her dress, which had slipped off one shoulder. Liz's fingers stiffened against the satiny fabric, for at the base of Penny's collarbone was a large bruise. Mottled and purple, it stained the white flesh. Liz drew a sharp breath.

Penny jerked away and righted her dress, eyes blazing. She shook her hair and snatched her hat from Naomi's hand. Seemingly incapable of speech, she spun around on her ridiculous heels and stormed out the door like a blue torpedo.

Silence hung in the room as everyone stared at the retreating presence. For his part, Beans sat placidly under the table.

The sound of Penny's heels on the staircase receded, and soon a door on the third floor—presumably Penny's—was slammed loud enough to be heard on the main floor. Caitlyn recovered first, and true to form her first concern was for Beans. She crouched by the table and reached for the dog. "Poor baby! Come on out. She's gone."

Liz let out a long-held breath. Then everyone began to talk at once.

"Serves her right! Coming in here and demanding to see our license!"

"Of all the nerve."

"Did you see that hat?"

"She's ruined our beautiful pie!"

No one, apparently, had seen the bruise except Liz. Penny's eyes had bored into Liz's face. She knew the mark had been exposed. And now Liz remembered what Sarah had said nearly a week ago when Penny had first arrived, about a bruise around Penny's eye.

What was happening to Penny? Was she simply clumsy, insisting on walking in shoes that feet were never intended to wear? Or was someone hurting her? Where did she go at night, coming in late, sometimes missing breakfast? The thought was sobering. Liz had felt little else but dislike for the interloping woman who was intent on causing trouble and flirting with Jackson every chance she got. Now, she wondered who Penelope Stryker really was and who might be harming her. And why?

Caitlyn had coaxed Beans out from under the table and was feeding him bits of pastry. The bulldog stopped nibbling briefly and raised wary eyes to his mistress. Liz leaned down with a distracted hand and patted his head. It was her fault, she supposed, for not making sure he was in her apartment with the door closed. Beans never could resist Mary Ann's strawberry-rhubarb pie.

"Good boy," she whispered. Beans had unearthed an unexpected clue. But a clue to what?

15

With Sarah's help, Liz had finished the morning's chores so that she and Naomi could get an early start for Bradyville. Outside the bakery, Liz tapped lightly on the horn and leaned back against the cool seat of her car. She hadn't slept well, her mind too busy for relaxation.

Naomi flung open the passenger door. "I'm sorry to have kept you waiting. I decided to pack up some more muffins for Lovina. With all she has to do caring for that sick woman, she probably doesn't have much time for baking."

It was so like Naomi to think of something like that. Liz was about to thank her for her thoughtfulness, but she was arrested by the sight of Penny Stryker's BMW pulling away from the inn. She showed up at the oddest times, times when Liz would expect her to be working. Like yesterday when she'd dropped in at Sew Welcome in the middle of the afternoon. And Liz had been pretty sure she had been outside in the foyer for a while before coming in. Had she been listening? Trying to catch them in some infraction of the rules? Just snooping? Liz had no idea.

"I guess the dragon lady will be a bit late for work today," Naomi observed.

Penny's BMW sped off toward Pleasant Creek's town hall. Recalling the ugly purplish bruise, Liz felt uneasy all over again.

"That was some scene she made yesterday," Naomi said. "That's twice she and Beans have tangled, and I think Penny lost on both counts." When Liz didn't respond, Naomi turned to face her. "What?

You don't think she'll make trouble for you, do you? I mean, sue you or the inn or something?"

"No, but . . ." She drew in a breath and let it out slowly. "I think she may have other problems."

"Like how to ensnare a mayor?" Naomi scoffed. "She's a fool to try. He's head over heels for you, and everyone knows it."

"I don't mean that." Liz turned onto the highway and lowered her voice, though they were alone. "I saw something when I tried to help her after she fell into the table."

"What did you see?"

"When I tried to straighten her dress, she winced in pain." Liz caught her lip in her teeth. "And I saw a big bruise between her shoulder and collarbone."

"Really? I didn't see it."

"I don't think anyone saw it but me, but she knew I saw it."

"So, she's clumsy," Naomi offered, playing devil's advocate. "Maybe she falls into other things besides tables. Little wonder, wearing shoes you have to climb a ladder to get into."

"Sarah told me she had a black eye covered with makeup the day she registered at the inn. You know how observant she is."

Naomi pondered the scene through her window a while. "What makes you think someone is deliberately hurting her? You can't tell that just from a bruise."

Liz shrugged. "It wasn't so much the bruise as the expression on her face when she knew I'd seen it."

They were both quiet as they sped down the highway. It was an awful thing to imagine, but Liz knew the statistics of battery, and knew how anger and frustration could lead to such behavior. Despite her dislike for Penny, she felt a wave of sympathy. No one should be mistreated like that.

"Lots of problems swirling around the Olde Mansion Inn," Naomi remarked at length. "I know you want to help, but some things are beyond our control." She glanced over her shoulder. "And there are some things that could get us in trouble too."

Liz knew she was thinking about the car that she had thought was following them the last time they'd visited Bradyville. It had come to nothing, and Liz had decided not to let it worry her, but she shivered anyway. More than one incident had made her wonder if someone might be watching her.

They found Lovina's aunt's house easily this time and pulled into the driveway. It took a while for a response to their knock, but finally the curtain next to the front door parted. Lovina's round face appeared. The deep-blue eyes showed anxiety mixed with recognition, and after the curtain dropped back in place, several seconds passed before the door slowly opened.

"Ms. Eckardt," Lovina said warily as she wiped her hands on her apron.

Liz smiled. "Please call us Naomi and Liz. We wanted to see you again. I hope it's all right." This conservative Amish household would not have a telephone, so it wasn't as though Liz could have called ahead of time anyway.

After a long pause, Lovina stepped back to usher them into the hushed parlor. "Come in." She stretched a hand toward two straight-backed chairs separated by a small table where they had sat on their previous visit.

"We brought you these," Naomi said, holding out the cake box she brought in. "Cinnamon streusel. We hope you like them."

"Oh—thank you." Lovina's eyes grew moist, and her lips trembled slightly.

It was a stronger reaction than the gift merited, and Liz feared that Lovina didn't have good news to share. They would likely hear that there had been no visit from the prodigal granddaughter. When Lovina continued her silence after settling into a chair across from them, Liz said, "I hope your aunt is better."

"Huldah will soon leave us," she said quietly. "But she is comfortable, and Gött is with her." She looked down at her lap and then at Liz with a scrutinizing gaze. "You brought me word of my *Grosstöchter*," she said. "And for that I thank you, but . . ." She seemed at a loss to continue. Something in her manner had changed. Was it simply the Amish reticence to mingle with Englishers? Or had her grandson warned her to avoid a certain busybody from Pleasant Creek?

"You have heard from Reece?" Liz asked eagerly.

The woman's expression brightened briefly before darting off to a space beyond Liz's head. "She came here to see me. She and Benedikt."

"Oh, that's wonderful," Liz said.

"It has been such a long time since I have seen my Grosstöchter," she said in a strained voice. Then she grew quiet again, the light in her face dissipating. "I had hoped to have a good long talk with her, but—" She broke off, and the lines around her mouth deepened. "My grandson was full of news about the farm and wanted to talk. He didn't give Reece a chance to speak."

Liz felt quick irritation. Surely he should have known how much Lovina would want to talk with Reece. He should have made himself scarce for a little while.

"Ben says everything is fine." Lovina twisted the fabric of her apron between her fingers and continued hesitantly. "I wanted to ask Reece—" She stopped and seemed to think better about divulging what she might have asked her granddaughter. "Maybe she worries that I am angry with her. I know she has departed from the faith of her childhood, but I will always love her. I want her to know that." Lovina broke off, as though shocked by her own confession to Englishers.

"I'm glad she was well enough to come," Liz said.

Lovina seemed puzzled. "She has been sick?"

"Ben told us she suffers from migraines, that she hasn't been feeling well."

Lovina's eyes darted away briefly, then returned to Liz and Naomi. She gazed at them as though she could discern truth in their faces. "She does. But her medication should help. I didn't know she was sick now."

"Ben said her migraine was very severe this time." Liz struggled with how much to say. "That's why we weren't able to see her at first when we went to your farm." Now it was Liz's turn to run out of words.

Lovina's brow furrowed. She seemed to ponder what to say. "My grandson is very private. He does not like to discuss family matters with outsiders. Only with the bishop. But you know, that is our way." She reddened, as though aware she might have given offense. She lowered her head. "I'm sorry if my grandson did not extend hospitality."

It was a plausible excuse for Ben's behavior, or might be if Ben were a practicing member of the Amish community, which he obviously was not.

A stricken expression passed over Lovina's face. She gripped the fabric of her apron. "I must talk to the bishop."

"Perhaps we should go," Naomi said in a small voice, nudging Liz with her elbow.

"I'm sorry to have upset you, Mrs. Hoffman," Liz said. She stood and extended her hand to Lovina. "It's just that we wanted to make sure Reece was all right, since she'd been ill, and to find out if you had seen her."

Lovina stood uncertainly and glanced from Liz to Naomi. Then quickly she walked to the door. "I thank you for your kindness—and the pastries." She stood, shuffling her feet in tiny, nervous steps, her lips pressed together. Then she spoke in a barely audible voice. "But it is best if you do not call or try to see Reece again."

Liz stared at the averted face. It was clearly a warning. What had happened? The tension was broken when a faint cry emanated from a room down the hall. "I must see to Huldah now," Lovina said, and closed the door abruptly behind them.

Neither spoke until Liz had driven away from the house and they were headed toward Pleasant Creek. "Sounds like we've worn out our welcome here too," Naomi said.

Liz was stunned by Lovina's words and by the desperate urging in them. What had changed since their earlier visit? She had been downright friendly and eager for news of Reece. This time she was cryptic, troubled, avoiding the gazes of her visitors as though afraid.

"I said, it appears we've worn out our welcome," Naomi repeated.

"Oh, I'm sorry. I was thinking." Liz hesitated and glanced warily into the rearview mirror.

"The road is clear behind us this time," Naomi said, observing Liz's nervousness. "But something's got you spooked."

"Lovina acted as though she was afraid of something," Liz said. "Or someone."

"She did seem nervous. Maybe she just didn't want anyone involved in their family affairs." Naomi released a long breath. "You know how the Amish are about that."

"Mmm," Liz mumbled. The Amish were a close-knit community, but this was different. Lovina had kept her voice low, almost as though she didn't want someone to hear. Her ailing relative? Or someone else? They'd seen no cars, but someone else could have been inside the house with them. She felt a coldness that made her shiver in stark contrast to the warmth inside the car.

Liz returned to the Olde Mansion Inn shortly after noon. She had asked Sarah to wait for her to change the linens in the rooms—a chore usually completed right after breakfast. They'd do it now before guests returned for coffee hour. She loved keeping the inn fresh and beautiful, and today she especially looked forward to working with her hands. She'd give the mysterious behavior of Lovina Hoffman a rest.

Beans met her at the door, wagging his stubby tail. She took him out for a quick walk and went in search of Sarah. She found her in the kitchen, placing a cheesecake in the refrigerator.

"All quiet on the home front?" she asked, warming to the sight of the always efficient Sarah in a dress of spring blue.

"Violet and Vera are quilting in the shop," Sarah said, straightening. "The Andersons left early this morning, and of course, Penny is at work. I've stacked sheets and towels on the hall table. Do you want some lunch before we get started? There's fresh bread, and ham and cheese in the refrigerator."

"No, let's get those rooms done before everyone comes back." Liz held the door open for Sarah, and they headed upstairs.

In a surprising spurt of energy, Beans left the comfort of his doggy bed. "You're coming up?" Liz asked him in surprise. For answer he heaved himself up the first two steps. "Okay, but you wait outside the guest doors like a good boy." She smiled, thinking Beans would probably not make it beyond the second stair. He apparently decided the effort was too great, backed himself down, then dropped like a lump on a rug on the rotunda floor.

Liz and Sarah changed the sheets in the Rose of Sharon Room first, for the Holmes sisters were the most likely to return early. A tidy pair, they always made their own beds with precision and tucked everything away. Liz noticed that the wastebasket by Violet's bed was filled with spent tissue, and she thought the pillow on the bed was slightly damp. Testaments to her unhappiness? Had Sadie had any luck in changing Vera's attitude toward Stefan? At least Violet had gotten out of bed today.

The Heirloom Room with its large four-poster bed was equally well ordered, though the Andersons had obviously made full use of the accommodations. Books were stacked in several places around the room, including the mantel of the carved fireplace, and the desk bore a stack of file folders and a variety of newspapers like the *Chicago Tribune* and *The Wall Street Journal*. Though the anniversary roses John had purchased for June filled the room with their heady fragrance, the air seemed to echo the struggle of the Andersons' business losses.

They'd left Penny's room for last. Her temporary boudoir was a chaos of clothes thrown across chairs and on the rumpled bed. The dresser and chests were cluttered with cosmetic containers, lipstick tubes, coins, and spent tissues. Hastily thrown-off shoes were scattered on the floor, and a pair of pink feathery slippers languished outside the bathroom door.

Liz stared in amazement. Penny's room wouldn't have won awards for neatness ever since she'd arrived, but this time was the worst she'd seen. "Yikes!" she said, turning to Sarah.

"Maybe she was in a terrible hurry this morning," Sarah answered with characteristic grace. She moved the shoes to the closet, but neither she nor Liz touched any of the personal items on the dresser or vanity. A guest could choose to live with a certain measure of abandon if she wished, but Liz hoped this kind of disorder was a one-off.

Liz gingerly moved the items of clothing to a nearby chair so she could change the sheets. She lifted the folds of a silky crimson gown and spotted a phone hidden beneath it.

"Penny will be missing this."

Sarah, who didn't use a cell phone—and rarely any kind of phone—simply stared over Liz's shoulder. *Careless living has its downside*, Liz thought. Penny would likely be returning for it soon.

She intended to set the phone on the cluttered bedside table but couldn't resist looking down at the device in its red alligator case.

Don't do it, her inner voice warned. *It's none of your business.* She made it a practice not to intrude on her guests' privacy, and to tinker with Penny's phone would certainly amount to that. Still, there might be a clue as to who was beating up on her. She grimaced and tapped the phone log button, indicating the last call made or received. No name appeared—just a local number. Probably a relative or friend, since most of Penny's business calls would be made from her office.

She started to put the phone down. Only . . . only there was something familiar about that number. Mentally, Liz repeated the digits of the call that had been made at 7:30 p.m. yesterday. And all the hairs on the back of her neck tingled. She had called that number herself several times trying to reach Reece Hoffman.

She turned to gaze into Sarah's wide eyes and breathed, "It's the number of the person who called asking for help. The person I believe was Reece Hoffman."

16

After helping Sarah serve coffee hour the following day, Liz retired to her quarters, her mind whirling with what she had learned—and with what remained hidden. Penny Stryker knew someone at the Hoffman farm. Reece? Ben? Mrs. Steele, the housekeeper? Penny had contacted someone there, and the conversation had lasted a full four minutes. What did Penny have to do with what was going on?

She hadn't seen Penny since the day of the accident in the sitting room when the purplish bruise on her collarbone had been exposed. She hadn't come down for breakfast the following morning or this morning. *Probably too embarrassed*, Liz thought, remembering how Penny's cold eyes, surrounded by a mask of eye shadow, had flashed with humiliation when she realized that Liz had seen the bruise.

Liz sat in her favorite chair with a cup of decaf coffee, glad to be alone with her troubling thoughts.

When her phone rang, Liz groaned, hoping it was a call she could ignore. But a glance at the screen changed her mind. "Jackson?" He rarely called at this time of day, when both of them were usually occupied with business.

"Hi, Liz. Sorry to bother you."

She brightened at the sound of his voice. "You never bother me."

"I'm sure you're busy, but have you seen Penny today?"

Penny? Taken aback, she didn't answer at first. "Um, no, actually. I haven't seen her since yesterday. She didn't come to the dining room for breakfast."

"Hmm." Jackson paused, then said, "She missed a meeting this morning, and apparently she's not answering her cell."

Was he worried about Penny? Or simply following up on an employee careless in the performance of her duties? Yesterday, her phone had been lying amid a clutter of discarded clothing on her bed. Had she gone off a second day without her phone? Or had she not returned to the inn last night? The behavior wasn't like Penny.

"Well, something must have come up, and this isn't the first time she's missed an appointment. When you see her, would you ask her to call in to the office?"

"Sure," she replied.

"You okay?" he asked.

"I'm fine," she replied absently.

"Take care, Liz." After a pause, he added, "I'll call you tonight."

She held the phone in her hand for a long moment after Jackson clicked off. So Penny hadn't exactly been the model employee. Where had she been since yesterday afternoon? Where was she now?

Liz recalled that Penny had an aunt living nearby. She'd never explained why she took up temporary residence at the Olde Mansion Inn instead of staying with this close relative. Liz had assumed she did so because she wanted to be close to the Pleasant Creek town hall.

She searched her memory for the name of the aunt, formerly of New York who had "moved in very elite circles." Margaret something. Cummings? Carruthers? Carstairs. Yes, that was it. Maybe Margaret Carstairs knew who Penny's contacts were, and who she might know in the Hoffman household.

She reluctantly lowered the footrest on her recliner, heaved herself up, and went to her computer. Beans followed at her heels, suddenly alert. It didn't take long to locate Margaret P. Carstairs. There was only one nearby, and she lived in the town of Reston.

What are the odds of that? Liz realized she might even have passed the woman's home on earlier visits to the farm. There had to be a connection, but what was it?

She jotted the address on a slip of paper without any clear idea of what she was going to do. Penny had given little information about her aunt. To explain her sudden return to the area to take up a temporary job, she had suggested she might be helpful to her older relative. Liz had believed that Jackson was the reason Penny had come to Pleasant Creek.

But maybe she'd been wrong.

She changed into clean jeans and a light sweater. She ran a brush through her hair, grabbed her purse, and headed to her car. It was nearly suppertime, and she would surely arrive in the middle of it with the drive. Not a good time to call, but if Margaret Carstairs was really one of those "elite" types, she might not dine until much later. In any case, she'd have to think of a plausible excuse for knocking at the woman's door.

Naomi had a huge order to get out in the next hour, and Sadie and Mary Ann were knee-deep in preparations for the city market. Despite the weird things that had been happening, she would go by herself, be careful, and hope for the best.

Her GPS led her to a handsome, aging house on the east side of Reston in what might once have been an upscale neighborhood. The homes on the street were beautiful old Victorian structures, colorful and covered in gingerbread trim. Some of the period houses were in the process of restoration, but the home connected to Margaret Carstairs had clearly been left to the vagaries of wind and weather. The house needed painting, the bushes needed trimming, but small pots of flowers on the carefully swept porch gave evidence of care.

Liz hesitated, noting the drawn shades and curtains, and climbed the steps to the front door. The stairs sagged and creaked with antiquity, and rust clung to the frame of the old-fashioned doorbell. She pressed it firmly.

Thirty seconds passed before the long curtain at the side of the door moved aside and an inquisitive face framed by tidy white hair looked out. The lady, appearing to be in her late seventies or early eighties, squinted through the glass. Seconds later, the door cracked slightly.

"If you're selling something, Miss, I don't need anything," she said with a pleasant half smile. She began to close the door.

"I'm not selling anything, Mrs. Carstairs. I'm a friend of your niece, Penelope." Liz swallowed against the little white lie. "My name is Liz Eckardt."

"Penny? You know Penny?" she asked, opening the door wider.

She was thin and delicate, wearing classic tailored trousers and a light-blue twinset sweater with white buttons. Pretty pearls graced her ears.

"Penny has been staying at the inn I own in Pleasant Creek. I wonder if I might come in, just for a few minutes."

Margaret Carstairs seemed to consider the wisdom of the idea, but sized Liz up and apparently did not assess her as a threat. She opened the door wider and stepped back to allow her caller entrance into the dusky living room, which was characterized by ornate antique furniture and a few photos and tasteful accent pieces. A brocade drape had been drawn over what appeared to be a grand piano, probably to keep the dust off it. Liz could almost smell the past settling over the house.

"Did she send you?" Mrs. Carstairs asked. "But where are my manners? Won't you sit down?" She indicated a Louis XV–style chair upholstered in a rococo floral jacquard print.

"Thank you," Liz said, liking this well-spoken lady and wishing she could put her at ease. But she felt far from comfortable herself. She searched her mind for a suitable opening. "You must be glad to see your niece after she's been away so long."

"Yes, I do miss her, although she can be exasperating." Margaret smiled. "But then, I probably shouldn't say that to you. Although, at my age, I tend to speak my mind."

Liz smiled back. "I know a few women who'd appreciate that—including me," she said, thinking of the Material Girls.

"So what can I do for you?" Margaret said. "Would you like tea?"

"No, please don't go to any trouble." Liz chided herself for not rehearsing in the car. She wasn't quite sure how to proceed, now that she was here.

The woman waited her out. Finally, Liz said, "I wondered if you had heard from Penny."

Margaret seemed to assess her. "So she didn't send you? To try to make up with me?"

Liz stared at her. This wasn't the answer she'd expected. Not that she knew *what* she'd expected. "Uh, no. The fact is, I'm a little worried about her."

Margaret rolled her eyes. "Let me guess. She hasn't shown up for work? Did she skip out on your bill?"

"Well, yes," Liz said, wondering where this was going. "And no. I mean, I did hear that she missed some meetings at the Pleasant Creek town hall. But I still have her credit card on file, so I'm not worried about the bill."

"If I were you, Ms. Eckardt, I'd run that card as soon as I got home. Now, perhaps I can set your mind at ease. Penny has a bad habit of landing good jobs—she can put on a very convincing show of competence—and then messing them up because she can't be bothered to show up when she's supposed to."

Liz didn't know what to say to that. "I didn't mean to imply—"

Margaret held up a hand. "No need to imply anything. I'm quite sure Penny is just fine, so you needn't worry."

"Do you know where she is? Has she contacted you?"

"No, but she'll turn up. She and I had a dreadful fight the last time she was here—she was livid that I'd sent some items on consignment over to the Pleasant Creek flea market. But she'll get over it."

Flea market? Liz leaned forward. There had to be a connection. "This is none of my business, but may I ask what the items were?" She held her breath.

Margaret shrugged. "I honestly don't know what the fuss was about—it was just some vintage clothes, a few old handbags, some old dishware, and an old, very ugly painting."

Liz drew in her breath. "A painting?"

"I'd never seen the thing before, just found it in the attic when I was clearing some things out for the dealer. But this is an old house, which belonged to my parents and grandparents before me. There are still plenty of nooks and crannies I haven't investigated."

Liz leaned forward in the old-fashioned chair. "I'm sorry," she said hesitantly, her mind thrumming. "If you don't mind telling me, what did it look like?"

"It was a dark, ugly thing—gnarly black trees against a gray sky. It makes me shiver just to think about it." She wore an expression of distaste. "I can't imagine why anyone ever saved such an unpleasant piece of art, let alone painted it in the first place."

Liz felt as though the wind were sucked from her chest. *That must have been the painting Sadie purchased from the flea market and later discovered had been stolen from Karl Anderson's Gold Coast shop in Chicago. Penny must somehow be involved in the ring of thieves the police were tracking.*

Margaret was staring at her. "What kind of trouble is my niece in?"

Liz shook herself mentally. "I-I honestly don't know," she stuttered. Liz thought about the black eye, the bruise on Penny's collarbone. "Can you tell me anything about her friends here in Reston—or in Pleasant Creek? Anyone she spends time with?"

Margaret was quiet for so long Liz wondered if she had heard. She was gazing into some place Liz couldn't see. It was clear she loved Penny, even though she knew Penny wasn't perfect. Finally, she spoke. "I don't know her friends. She doesn't confide in me. I offered her a place here when she told me she would be in town, but after the fuss about the painting she hasn't come back."

Liz rose and fumbled in her purse for a business card, which she handed to Margaret. "If you hear from Penny, would you call me?"

Margaret also stood, then looked meaningfully at Liz. She picked up a pen and a piece of note paper from the table next to her chair, and scribbled something on it. "Here's my number. I'd appreciate it if you would also call when you catch up with her." Margaret extended her hand to Liz. "Of course we're angry at each other, but we're flesh and blood."

She showed Liz to the door.

Liz's mind raced as she pulled out of Margaret's driveway. Was Penny just a bit player in whatever nefarious schemes were going on, trying to make a quick buck with a valuable painting?

Or was she in a starring role?

The sun was rapidly setting in a hazy spring sky as Liz drove back toward the highway. She shivered and turned up the heat. Her talk with Mrs. Carstairs had left her unsettled. She hadn't trusted Penny from the first moment they'd met because of the way she flirted with Jackson, but she hadn't guessed the outrageous woman might be mixed up in burglary. Someone—almost certainly the young man Sadie had said tried to grab the painting from her—must have seen Sadie pick it up at the flea market. He'd waited until she stowed it in the Jeep, then he stole the whole car to get at what he really wanted. He must be working for this stolen art ring too.

Almost without realizing it, Liz found herself on the county road south of Reston—the road she knew would lead to the Hoffman farm. It was risky to go there again, but she had to find out what Penny's connection was.

She drove to the snaky road she remembered from former visits. The vegetation on both sides of the road seemed even thicker now. Before reaching the clearing where she knew the farm lay shrouded in dusk, she slowed to a near stop and cut all but the parking lights. Ahead was the iron gate, closed and padlocked.

She tested the ground at the edge of the road, which seemed hard enough to keep the tires from sinking in, then veered into the heavy brush. She stopped the car near a stand of thick-leaved trees. Here her car could not be seen from the house and probably wouldn't be noticed by another vehicle passing by. She felt her nerves jump as she set the parking brake. She knew she ought to turn around and go back, but if she could just have a quick look around . . .

Liz knew that Chief Houghton was working on the case involving the stolen art, along with other high-end antique thefts. He'd been in contact with other city officials and police departments, including the prickly but seemingly competent Rex Bladen of Reston. If there was something to be found here, the authorities would find it. But had they taken her suspicions of Ben Hoffman seriously? She remembered the chief's warning. *You're not getting in over your head on this one, are you?*

What had possessed her to come here? She could hardly walk up to the house, knock on the door and say, "I was in the neighborhood." Still, some inner compulsion urged her on.

She closed the car door carefully and edged toward the farm, easily stepping over the iron gate. As she approached, she became aware of movement. She heard muffled clunks and scrapes and low voices. Why would men be working at night and what would they be doing? Caring for the livestock perhaps, though she had seen no cows or horses on her earlier visits, only a few chickens foraging about near the house.

She crouched low behind clumps of wild grass and rogue bushes, and listened. An idling engine droned, but no light shone through the thick foliage. Not even the light of the moon. The noises seemed to be coming from the fenced-in building where she and Sadie had encountered the snarling dog. But the beast, if he was there, was making no sound.

What if the Hoffman farm was being used as a holding area for stolen goods? It was a perfect hideout—remote, unremarkable. Who would suspect a quiet farm run by an Amish widow—a widow who was conveniently off the premises and unlikely to return for a while? Liz crept closer, glad she had chosen to wear the black nylon jacket instead of her yellow one. Sneakers would have made for easier trekking, but the ankle boots she had chosen at least provided protection from the thorny underbrush, and it wasn't like she'd planned this little adventure when she left Pleasant Creek earlier.

A few hundred yards ahead, the double gate of the shed was open. A large box truck idled near it. The sound of men moving about grew in intensity, the unrecognizable voices becoming louder. Two men in dark clothing carried large crates from the shed to the truck, grunting as they hefted them into the vehicle. A third man—who seemed to be in charge—stood watching the men work, issuing instructions in a low, urgent voice.

Liz pushed forward, creeping past a smaller shed and closing the distance between herself and the activity in progress. She crouched at the rear of the fenced-in building, her breath coming in short, quick gasps. She knew that third man's voice even before she identified his muscular frame and ruddy face. Benedikt Hoffman.

"Step it up," he ordered. "I want this place cleared fast. Rex can't hold them off much longer."

Liz pressed herself against the rough wood of the fence and clamped a hand over her mouth to smother her gasp. What they were loading had nothing to do with farm equipment or crops and everything to do with whatever they had been keeping hidden. And the new police chief, Rex Bladen, was part of it. It was instantly clear to her. She had been right to distrust Ben. Lovina's farm was being used to hold stolen merchandise, and Ben knew the authorities were getting close to discovering the truth. Liz herself had probably played some part in tipping him off, though, of course, she hadn't done it on purpose. She could only hope her nosing around hadn't jeopardized the chief's investigation—or worse, gotten anyone hurt.

She had to call Stan Houghton. She'd have to leave without knowing what was happening to Reece, but hoped the police would get here in time to save her—if she needed saving and hadn't been part of the scheme all along. The thought didn't sit well with her, but it had to be entertained.

Liz scrambled to extract her phone from her pocket without standing up and exposing her presence. She closed her fingers around it and struggled to free it from the folds of fabric stretched tight across her hips. She almost had it when something jabbed into her back and a sharp voice, heavy with sarcasm, broke the silence.

"Well, if it isn't Little Miss Innkeeper! Fancy meeting you here!"

17

Liz whirled around. She saw a slim figure in dark clothes and a baseball cap, holding a gun. "Penny!" Liz exclaimed, staring into the cold blue eyes leveled on her. Gone were the cloud of platinum hair, the makeup, and the fancy feminine clothes. Black sneakers replaced the four-inch stilettos. She stood eye-to-eye with Liz, dark and threatening.

"Yes, it's me." She waved the gun menacingly. "You just couldn't leave it alone, could you? Just had to keep picking at it and trying to ruin everything. I don't know what Jackson sees in you," she spat through teeth that gleamed in the faint light of the moon. "Now turn around! Walk straight ahead and don't make any sudden moves." Then her sharp voice rose in a shout. "Ben! We've got a visitor."

Liz moved—one foot, then the other—toward the little group around the white box truck. The two men who were loading crates stopped, sweaty faces puzzled. Ben glared in her direction but stood waiting for her to approach. Penny jabbed her prisoner onward. Suddenly, Liz's phone sounded from inside her pocket. Why hadn't she thought to mute it or set it to vibrate? If only she could answer and advise whoever it was of the danger she faced.

"Give it here!" Penny demanded at the sound, pushing the muzzle of the gun deeper into her back.

Reluctantly, Liz withdrew her phone, which Penny snatched away.

Liz walked obediently toward Ben's tall, imposing form. He stood with his arms crossed over his chest. His eyes were smoldering coals. "Just happened by?" he asked with smooth irony. "Have a suitcase to return?"

Liz steadied herself, not flinching from his intrusive scowl. "Just a concerned citizen," she replied evenly, "wanting to know what you have done with Reece."

"Ah, my little cousin—the start of all this trouble," he said. "She and other nosy people who don't mind their own business." He glared at Liz, then jerked his head to Penny. He held out a hand for the gun.

Liz didn't miss the look of fear on Penny's features or the trembling hand that released the weapon. Clearly, Penny was part of the nefarious dealings goings on, but she seemed like a pawn or an employee—and a very nervous one. Was Ben the one who had inflicted her bruises? And where was Reece? Liz felt her anger rising despite the fear gripping her heart. "You been beating up on *her* too?" she asked the glowering man.

His dark eyes flickered as the words hit their mark, but he stood his ground, the gun poised in his left hand. He glared at the men standing agape at the truck. "What are you waiting for? Keep loading!"

"You won't get away with this," Liz said with fire that surprised her. "The police have been watching you." Ben had to know this, which was why he was working under cover of darkness to get rid of the evidence. She was aware of the men continuing to move large canvas-draped items along with crates that likely contained smaller valuable items. "How could you do this to your own family?" she demanded, thinking of the unsuspecting Lovina gently caring for a dying woman with the compassion that was second nature to the Amish.

The harsh lips twitched as Liz's accusation stung the air. He took a deep breath and lifted his square jaw. "There was never any need for unpleasantness," he said in a flat, conciliatory tone. Then his nostrils flared as he added, "If my cousin had minded her own business and hadn't mouthed off to some stranger. We just needed a little time and we'd have been out of here with no one getting hurt."

"No unpleasantness?" she shot back. "No one hurt? What about the people you've been stealing from?"

Ben raised the gun and pointed it in her direction. "I don't need any sermons from you. It's a dog-eat-dog world, and I'm tired of living on scraps! And I'm tired of interfering do-gooders." He shoved the gun into Penny's hand. "Take her to the house and lock her up until we're finished here. And no slipups this time!"

"You heard Ben. Get going." Penny waved Liz forward with the gun.

Liz walked to the shadowy farmhouse, trying not to think about what might lie ahead. She listened for the sound of the big dog that had nearly devoured her and Sadie, but all was quiet except for the men's rushing feet as they continued to load the truck.

"Go on in. It isn't locked."

Liz pushed open the door but hesitated on the threshold.

"Inside!" Penny prodded, her voice rising in intensity. "Upstairs!"

The hall and parlor in the Amish farmhouse were deserted. It wasn't wired for electricity, and there was no telltale scent of kerosene. A dim light glowed from the second-floor landing. The current occupants of the house most likely depended on battery-driven devices like the camping lantern Liz glimpsed as she approached the top of the uncarpeted stairs.

A door opened and Mrs. Steele stood in the opening, her gaunt face tightly controlled but pale as milk. Slate-gray eyes widened in the furrowed face, the smaller eye drooping oddly. She wore the same brown dress buttoned down the front of her tall, oppressively spare figure. Her thin lips parted, but no sound emerged. She backed up to admit them, and Penny nudged Liz inside.

Someone sprang up from the end of a quilt-covered bed. "Liz!" came a quivery voice. Reece took a few steps forward, joy and relief spreading over her ashen face. Her hair was disheveled, and she'd clearly been crying. Reece glanced at the gun in Penny's hand, then whispered, "Liz, you—you shouldn't have come!" The words belied the relief in her features.

"Are you all right?" Liz asked, reaching for one of Reece's hands. The lovely French nails she remembered from the plane were torn and ragged, and dark shadows ringed the girl's eyes. "I've been so worried about you. So has your grandmother."

"I didn't think you'd ever find me," she said in a trembling voice. "I kept hoping you wouldn't give up on me."

"This is all very cozy, I'm sure," Penny said. "You—over there," she told Liz, waving the gun toward a rocking chair. "And you, Miss New York model, get back where you were and sit down." She turned to Mrs. Steele. "Take Liz's purse, and make sure you get her car keys. Here's her phone. I'll see to these two. Ben wants you to bring some sandwiches. The men worked through supper."

The housekeeper—or jailer, as the case might be—did as she was told. She grabbed Liz's bag, dropped the phone inside it, then frisked her, pulling her keys out of Liz's jacket pocket. She cast a disturbed glance at them all and hurried from the room, taking Liz's things and closing the door behind her.

"So, what happens now?" Liz demanded when she had dropped down on the bare wooden rocker. Torn between relief that Reece was apparently okay and fear of what might transpire in the next few moments, she stared at Penny with what she hoped was defiance.

"We wait till Ben says it's time to go," Penny said, thrusting her chin forward. Bright strands of her thick platinum hair spilled out from beneath the baseball cap, and her face, bare of makeup, revealed a spray of freckles and sunspots.

"Do you always do what Ben says?" Liz asked with quiet directness. "How'd you get mixed up with him in the first place?"

"I've known him since we were kids, as if it's any of your business.

Then again, clearly that doesn't stop you. Anyway, we're all going to be rich." She sidestepped to the window and peered out. Turning back, she gave a little giggle. "Well, not *all* of us. There are other plans for Reece here—and I'm sure Ben will cook up something special for you, Liz."

Liz shot Reece what she hoped was an encouraging glance. She raised an eyebrow at Penny, who was so tense, she seemed about to spring. "You do what he says because you think he's going to share what he gets with you," Liz said. "Or maybe you bow and scrape because if you don't, he'll beat you up again. You don't have to take that. No one should—"

"Shut up!" Penny shot back. She peered through the window once more, scowling. "It's all Aunt Margaret's fault. If she hadn't found the painting I hid at her house and given it to that flea market dealer, Ben and that woman would never know that I kept it for myself after the job. That's what made them mad."

Them? That woman? Was Mrs. Steele more than just an employee? She certainly looked the part. Liz peered into Penny's face as though the answer might reveal itself.

Penny suddenly shook her hair free in a gesture of triumph. "But I got it back and they forgave me. I wasn't about to let that white-haired friend of yours get it. Ben said I was clever to swipe her Jeep."

Liz felt the puzzle pieces click into place. It had been Penny with Sadie in the flea market. Sadie had said there was something familiar about Penny. *I don't mean long-ago familiar. I've seen that face somewhere lately.*

Disguised as a man, Penny had been the one reaching for the painting.

Reece, who had been sitting quietly on a wicker trunk, seemed to find some gumption and pointed at Penny. "Ben's not going to take you with him. When he's through, he'll just throw you away," she said. "He won't share his profits with anyone if he doesn't have to. He's never been the generous type."

"You don't know anything!" Penny shot back angrily.

"I know my cousin, and he doesn't care about anyone but himself," Reece said flatly.

"We could have cut you in, remember? Ben wanted to, but no, you had to go all holier than thou on us. You two are the ones who will get tossed out." She grabbed a key from the pocket of her jeans and held it up in the air. "But not until they say so." Wagging the gun, she backed out of the room and turned the key in the lock with a click that echoed around the walls.

Liz crossed the room to join Reece. "Are you sure you're okay?" she asked, closely examining the young woman, who sat with her arms wrapped around her knees. Who knew what she'd been through in the past week or so since they'd met on the plane?

"They didn't hurt me," she said softly. "At first things were okay, even though Ben wouldn't let me leave to go visit Grossmutter. Ben showed me around the farm, and I enjoyed seeing my old *Haus* and going through some of the things Grossmutter saved from my childhood." A little sob caught in her throat. "He kept promising to drive over to Bradyville with me to see her. But on the third day, I realized he was into something bad." She shook her head sadly. "I heard commotion at night, and men coming and going. I—I saw what they were putting in the barn."

"Stolen antiques and valuable art," Liz supplied.

"Yes. They were using our farm to hoard them. I told my cousin he had to stop, but he wouldn't listen to me." She dropped her head onto her arms. "Grossmutter would be devastated if she knew, especially since he's her grandson and he's misusing her farm, the family's farm. At first, I pretended that it didn't matter, that I wouldn't say anything, but I—I couldn't go along with it. I couldn't do that to her. When I threatened to expose what he was doing, he had me locked in here.

That's when I called you with a phone I hid from him in my luggage. Of course, he confiscated that too when he found out."

"But he took you to see your grandmother," Liz said.

"After you wouldn't give up and kept trying to see me, they had to make it seem like everything was fine here, that I was fine. It was so hard to pretend with her. And of course, he was watching and listening the whole time. I couldn't get word to her—or to anyone else about what was happening."

"I'm so sorry, Reece," Liz said, drawing her arm around the girl's shoulders. "I can't imagine what it must feel like to be held prisoner by your own cousin."

"That new sheriff has been here too. He's dirty, Liz. He's in on the whole thing."

"I know," she said softly.

"And there's someone else too. An older woman. I don't know who she is, but I've seen her with Ben out by the barn. My cousin acts like he's almost afraid of her."

Penny had referred to someone as "that woman" and said "they" had plans. An older woman? A woman besides Penny was involved in all of this. After a long moment, Liz said, "We've got to find a way to get out of here. Besides, who knows—" Liz broke off, not wanting to scare Reece further. Ben and his crew might not hesitate to use a gun for something besides scare tactics. She grasped Reece's arm, trying to banish her own fear. "We won't let them get away with this."

Liz had to find a way to get out and get help. But how?

18

Liz had no idea how long she and Reece waited in the gathering dark, jumping at the slightest sounds and racking their brains about how they might get out of this situation alive. Time was running out. Ben and his crew seemed desperate to remove evidence from Lovina Hoffman's remote farm where they had been storing the stolen antiques and jewelry.

They would also be desperate to silence the two women who had witnessed their activities. The prospect sent a shiver up her spine and finally galvanized her into action.

She squeezed Reece's hand and went to check the room's only window. It was nailed shut from the outside, not that she'd expected it to be that easy.

"I got away once," Reece said, coming to look over Liz's shoulder. "I got about thirty feet down the back slope when Ben caught me. Well, Ben and that animal that guards the shed at night."

The dog, wherever it was out there, hardly registered as a concern right now. She had to figure out how to escape. She searched the plain upstairs room for some implement that might prove useful. But the wardrobe and the old walnut dresser in the corner had been cleared of all but a few worn linens.

"Mrs. Steele went through my suitcase too," Reece said. "She took everything but my clothes and my toothbrush. What are we going to do?"

"There must be a way," she mumbled, staring at the door.

"Before they took my cosmetic case, I tried jimmying the lock with my nail file and even my comb, but it was no use. And we may be alone now, but we can't count on one of them not coming back. Mrs. Steele and Penny both come and go. I don't think Ben's ever laid a hand on Mrs. Steele—I think he's even a little afraid of her. He gets angry and takes it out on Penny."

Liz thought of the black eye and the purple bruise on Penny's shoulder. How could a man who had been reared to hold life as sacred turn into a brute who battered another person into submission? And how had Ben been able to hide his real colors from his grandmother? But there was no time for speculation or regret. She pointed to what looked like a window in the ceiling that had been framed and painted over. "Reece, what do you suppose that is? Up there in the drywall?"

"Grossmutter used this bedroom for storage when I lived here. I seldom entered it. But I think it might be an opening into the attic."

"Which just may have a window to the outside," Liz said, excitement growing.

"But how would we get up there?" Reece grimaced. "And who knows what might be lurking inside? Mice or bats or—" She cringed and wrapped her arms around herself. "But I'll go through just about anything to get out of here."

Liz stared at the old dresser, then at the wicker trunk. If they could put the trunk on top of the dresser, it might just be high enough. She glanced around the room. There didn't seem to be any other options. "Quick, help me push the dresser. No, wait. Can we lift it so it makes less noise?"

Straining to hear sounds from the first floor and outside their door that would indicate they were about to be discovered, they each took a corner of the dresser and heaved. The Amish-made furniture was substantially built, and it was heavy. There was no way they were going to carry it.

"Set it down gently," Liz whispered. When it was on the floor again, Liz pulled out a drawer. "Put these on the floor." Reece nodded her understanding, and took the drawers as Liz handed them to her, then set them down without a sound.

Without the extra weight, they managed to position the dresser under the opening. Liz inclined her head toward the trunk. Silently, the two women moved toward it, then each took a handle and hefted the box on top of the dresser. It added enough height that they'd be able to reach the opening.

She could only hope they didn't fall and break their necks before they could enact phase one of their escape.

"Ready?" Liz whispered. "I'll go first."

Liz took a deep breath, then climbed onto the bed, which gave a sharp creak. She froze, as did Reece. After a minute that felt like an hour, it appeared that no one was coming to check on the noise. Reece steadied the dresser as Liz climbed onto its sturdy flat top, then up onto her knees on the wicker basket, praying that the woven twigs would hold her weight. There would be no one to hold the dresser for Reece, but Reece was lighter, younger, and probably a great deal more agile than Liz. And there might even be something in the attic—a rope or maybe even a ladder—that Liz could use to help.

Liz looked down at Reece from her precarious perch, then, feeling slightly dizzy, looked quickly back up. She wasn't afraid of heights, but in her current situation she probably should be. She gave the door, which was only about three feet above her head, a gentle push, then a harder shove to break the paint sealing it shut.

Finally, it moved, and a whiff of musty air filled her nostrils. She fought back a sneeze, then pressed the door up again and slid it to the left, opening a square of blackness in the ceiling.

Liz drew up into a squat and grabbed the edge of the frame. She pulled herself up and inside the hole, being careful not to press off too hard with her feet so the tower didn't go crashing to the floor. A bright moon shone through a window in one gable end of the house, and ambient light from the room below gave some relief from the darkness. Liz, lying on the floor of the attic and deliberately not thinking about what her clothes were now covered in, placed her face over the opening. "Can you do it by yourself or should I hunt for something to help you?" she whispered.

Reece shook her head. "I can do it."

And she did, somehow managing to not tip over their makeshift ladder. Liz reached out a hand to help pull her into the attic. "Come on. Quickly, before someone comes back."

Waiting a moment until their eyes adjusted to the dim light, they made their way along one of the floor joists—in this old house, there was probably good reason not to trust the ragged patches of flooring—toward the window. It wasn't more than fifteen inches wide and about as tall. It would be a tight squeeze, but it led onto a sharply sloping roof. They'd have to try to slide down it and get safely to the ground. Liz gasped when she felt something crawl across her foot.

"You okay?" Reece whispered.

"Yes," she said, gritting her teeth. "Let's go."

The window was attached by old-fashioned hinges that enabled it to swing outward. In less than thirty seconds Liz had pushed through it. She crouched down on the roof, working to maintain her balance as Reece crept out after her. They were at the back of the farmhouse, which faced the woods—a fortuitous tangle of brush and pine camouflage, and the opposite side of the house from the barn where all the illegal activity was happening. And the vicious dog. If they were lucky, they might just make it to her car.

No, we will *make it,* she resolved, *one step at a time.* Somehow, without a phone, they had to get word to the authorities before all the evidence of the thefts was removed. Liz slid down the slanted roof and peered over the edge. She grimaced. Before she lost her nerve, she carefully lowered herself over the side until she hung by her fingertips and dropped to the ground with a thud. It wasn't a fun landing, but nothing felt broken. Reece followed. Liz glanced around, making sure no one had heard them, and helped her to her feet. Together, they fled toward the trees.

It was fully dark in the dense woods behind the farmhouse. Reece stumbled along in her clog-style slippers, the only footwear her captors had left in the room after her things had been confiscated. If she removed them to run, she could do serious damage to her feet in the dark bracken. Liz grasped her hand and pulled her along, grateful for the occasional glimpse of moonlight through the leafy expanse. "You can do this," Liz urged.

"Where are we going?" Reece groaned between strangled gasps for breath. "Does anyone know where we are?"

Liz could have kicked herself for not leaving a note at home, for not telling someone where she was going. She had simply jumped in her car and headed for Margaret Carstairs's residence, without thinking it through, just because she thought she had a lead. *You'd think I'd learn.* She had started out late in the afternoon and spent more time there than she'd planned. The drive from Margaret's house to the farm had consumed the last of the light, and now they ran through the darkness at the mercy of desperate criminals who couldn't afford to let them get away.

An engine roared to life in the distance and struck new fear in Liz's heart. Urgent voices wafted on the quiet air, and the sound of rushing feet echoed through the woods. Their escape had been discovered. They would be pursued. Liz tried to pinpoint in her mind the location of her car, which she had parked under a covering of trees beyond the gate.

Mrs. Steele had taken her purse and keys, but Liz had an ace in the hole—a magnetic key box hidden under the passenger side rear wheel well. She'd had it since she'd lived in Boston and discovered once how expensive it was to have a locksmith open her car when she locked her keys inside. It might just save them—if they could reach it in time. Were they even running in the right direction?

By now Jackson would have called her, wondering where she was and why she was late for dinner. What would he think when she didn't answer? Perhaps he would assume she was busy with her guests and decide to try a little later. Or would he guess something was wrong and—miracle of miracles—be searching for her right now? But what if he thought she was angry with him over something and decided to give her space, the last thing in the world she wanted from him right now? How she longed to be with him and her friends, instead of running like a crazed rabbit from a bunch of dangerous thieves.

Chief Houghton's admonition rang in her mind. She was in way over her head after all—and so was Reece. Ben and his cohorts couldn't afford to let them escape. But they also couldn't afford to remain here with the evidence. Maybe Ben would send the truck on and remain to dispose of the interlopers. She didn't want to think about the pistol that might be trained on them at this very moment.

Liz saw a clearing ahead. They were almost to the edge of the woods. "Get down!" she rasped, tugging Reece's hand until they were crouched behind a tangled clump of bushes intertwined with tall weeds and spreading vines. Lungs bursting, arms and legs trembling, they waited. "We'll rest for just a minute, catch our breath, and then we'll make a break for the gate."

Long seconds passed. The engine noise had stopped, as had the voices. Only the cicadas and the wheezing of their overstressed lungs broke the stillness. "Now!" Liz whispered. They sprinted to the gate, clambered over it and ran toward the stand of trees where she had left the car. Just a few feet to go. They were going to make it!

Liz raced to the rear of the car and jammed her hand over the wheel and up into the space above it, feeling for the magnetic box. Her fingers probed the cold metal, which was damp with evening dew. Where was it? It had to be here. It had to—

A light flashed, momentarily blinding her. A strident voice broke the air and a figure leaped forward from the cover of trees.

"Looking for this?" Penny Stryker stood grinning with the gun in her right hand. She dropped the flashlight and pulled Liz's spare key from her pocket, dangling the ring from her finger.

19

Liz gaped in horror through the ambient glow of Penny's flashlight, which now illuminated a path from Penny to Liz and Reece. Somehow, Penny had found the car and gotten the key first, although it probably hadn't been that hard. Penny would have known Liz wouldn't trek too far to get to the farmhouse, so the car had to be somewhere nearby. Even Penny's thinking to look for a magnetic key box wasn't that big a stretch. She was a thief, and she associated with thieves. Surely she was used to eliminating backup plans.

Liz drew in her breath, struggling for calm. "So, what do you plan to do now?" She hoped she sounded defiant, though that certainly wasn't how she felt. Her insides quivered. Reece stood stock-still beside her.

For answer, Penny pocketed the key, then pulled out a phone and tapped the screen. "I've got 'em!" she yelled into the phone. "You can call off the manhunt."

"You won't get away with this," Liz said. "The police are on to you. They're on their way right now," she bluffed.

"Shut up!" Penny shouted. "You're lying, and you and I both know it. If the police were on their way, you wouldn't have come out here by yourself and gotten caught." If Liz had to bet, she'd say Penny didn't have it in her to shoot anyone. But the way that gun was wobbling as her hand shook, there was no guarantee it wouldn't go off unintentionally.

Reece seemed to shake off some of her fear, because she found her voice. "Why are you doing this, Penny? You know Ben doesn't have any loyalty to anyone but himself. When you get caught—and you will—he'll find a way to pin everything on you."

Penny aimed the gun toward Reece. It was clear her arm was beginning to tire because the gun was now held at a less than ninety-degree angle. "Well, look who's talking. You can just shut up again, Supermodel. You think I trust him? How stupid do you think I am?"

Liz would have loved to answer that question. Anybody who'd get mixed up in a mess like this and expect to get away with it might not be stupid, but was either supremely arrogant or had a screw loose. Maybe both.

"Penny," Liz said, trying for a reasonable tone, "there's time before whoever you called gets here. You could give me the keys and we could all drive away from here, right now. If we go straight to the police and you tell them your story, help them catch Benedikt and the rest of the gang, there's a very good chance you can walk away from this with nothing more than a charge for stealing Sadie's Jeep. You might not even get prison time, if Sadie decides not to press charges." Of course that was highly unlikely given Sadie's love for her Jeep, but Penny didn't have to know that. "You know this can't last. They'll get caught eventually. It's hard to fence unique things like genuine art. Sooner or later, someone will slip up. You don't have to go down with the rest of them."

Penny hesitated, just for a moment. Just long enough for Liz to see that she was thinking about it.

"What's in this for you, anyway?" Reece said, her voice growing stronger. "If I know Ben, he's planning to cut you out of any deal you made. Liz is right. Let's get in the car and drive away from here."

Penny steeled herself. "Ben's an underling, just like me, which you well know. *She's* in charge. She's the one who told him he could knock me around."

Mrs. Steele. Reece *had* said Ben was afraid of her. Was the housekeeper the mastermind behind this whole scheme?

But time was running out. Once Benedikt, or Mrs. Steele, or whoever Penny had called got here—and it couldn't be long now—it would be too late. It might already be too late for the stolen goods, which could already be rolling along to wherever stolen goods went to be sold. At least Liz could give a good description of the van—if she survived long enough to *give* a description.

Penny's arm was drooping again. Sadie had given Liz some shooting lessons, and Liz had been surprised to learn how quickly muscles fatigued in that position.

She was just about to make her move when Reece shouted, "I see flashing lights in the distance! The police are here!"

Penny turned, and Liz lunged at the other woman, catching her in the back with her shoulder. Penny's arm flailed, and the gun went flying into the bushes. Liz tackled her. Penny lay facedown on the cold, wet ground, grunting and struggling. Liz dropped on top of her and pinned her down.

Reece called out, "I can't find the gun!"

"Never mind that," Liz wheezed. "How close are the police cars?"

Reece appeared next to Liz, then sat down hard on Penny's legs. "I didn't see any. I lied to distract her."

Penny struggled and squirmed, but she was no match for the two women. Liz was able to catch her breath long enough to say, "Reach into her pocket while I hold her. Get the keys and start the car. We have to—"

"Have to what, Liz? Die?"

That voice. Liz knew it, but in her struggle to hold down Penny, it didn't register immediately.

"Get them off Penny," she ordered. Liz felt beefy hands grab her arms from behind and haul her to her feet, then hold her in a vicelike grip. Before the thug even turned her around to face the mastermind, Liz realized who the voice belonged to.

When her captor set her down on her feet, still holding her from behind, Liz stared into a face she knew.

"June Anderson?" she said, still not quite believing what she'd heard, even as she now saw the proof.

Her guest gave a sardonic laugh as Reece and Penny were hauled to their feet. Benedikt held Reece.

Penny brushed herself off and jabbed a finger into Liz's chest. "You're going to pay for that little stunt," she hissed.

Liz ignored her. Penny was the least of her problems right now. "June, seriously? You and Karl are running a stolen art ring? Do your sons know?"

June rolled her eyes. "You've got to be kidding. Dear stupid Karl doesn't know a thing, and neither do my boys. And we're going to keep it that way."

"How do you think you're going to do that?" Liz said, not bothering to struggle against the arms that held her. It would be better to conserve what energy she had left. "You know there's a police investigation, right? It's only a matter of time until you're caught."

"Let's just say I have friends in high places," June said. She pulled out her cell phone.

"Who? That crooked sheriff, Rex Bladen? He's small potatoes. You've transported stolen goods across state lines. The FBI will eat you and the rest of your crew alive."

June's face hardened. She punched a number into the phone. "Get that panel van over here. *Now.*" She smiled at Liz. "You talk a good game. But you and your little friend here are going for a ride—across state lines, if you'd like to know. And the only way you're coming back is in a couple of caskets."

Reece, who had been silent up till now, spoke up. "I see flashing lights."

Liz tried not to groan. Surely Reece was smarter than to try that again—although it had worked beautifully the first time, causing enough distraction that Liz had been able to get the drop on Penny. Not that it had done them any good in the long run. June's goons had them locked up tight.

This time Penny rolled her eyes. "We're not falling for that again."

"Penny, shut up," June ordered. "If you'd done your job in the first place and hadn't tried to cheat me out of that painting, we wouldn't be experiencing this delay right now." She looked at the display on her cell phone. "Where are those idiots? How long does it take to drive a van less than a mile?"

Liz looked past June to the road beyond. A car's headlights were visible in the distance.

But they weren't coming from the direction of the farm.

"June!" Benedikt yelled. "That can't be the van. Someone is actually coming."

"Move it!" she ordered. "Penny, give Ben the car keys. Ben, Joe, put those two in the back seat and hit the child locks. Ben, start driving. Take them out to the landfill. I'll have the van meet you there. Now go!"

Liz wasn't going without a struggle. As Joe pushed her toward the car, she dug in her heels, dragging her feet. Then she donkey-kicked his shins as hard as she could. The blow must have hurt, or at least startled him, because he released his grip a fraction, just long enough for Liz to break free. She made a run for the road, waving her arms. Ben ran after her, but she'd bought enough time.

Blue and red lights flashed as the oncoming car sped toward them, and a siren began to wail.

From the shoulder of the road, Liz continued waving. She turned around long enough to see figures—Penny, June, Joe, and Ben—running in different directions into the woods.

The police car careened to a stop and Liz raced toward the vehicle. Stan Houghton and Officer Jack Gerst jumped out. "Backup's on the way, Liz," he said as Reece reached them, limping a little. She'd kicked off the slippers and was now barefoot.

"And I'm here too, Liz," a familiar voice called as its owner stepped out of the back seat. A second police car, then a third fell into line and officers started into the woods at the chief's commands.

Liz fell into Jackson's arms, exhausted.

20

Colorful booths lined the downtown streets as tourists and residents of Pleasant Creek flocked to the town market. Every shop and organization in Pleasant Creek had gone all out to support the event. Sunshine spilled from a cloudless sky and light breezes stirred the spring air.

Liz breathed in the friendly atmosphere, the harrowing events of the night before calmed—but not forgotten. With Jackson gently propelling her through the maze, she headed for Sew Welcome's booth where she knew her friends would be waiting for her. When they got there, Sadie and the rest of the Material Girls flooded out, except Mary Ann, who waved from the interior, where she was waiting on a customer.

Sadie flung her strong arms around Liz and squeezed her tight. "You are a sight for sore eyes." She pulled Liz in and toward the rear of the booth where chairs had been set up.

"You know better than to go off by yourself," Naomi scolded, though her words had no bite.

"Point taken, and I'm so sorry to have worried you all. I don't know what made me go back to that farm, except that I was so worried about Reece."

Vera and Violet came around the corner of the booth, sparing her from having to continue to apologize for putting herself in danger. The sisters' faces were wreathed in smiles—and holding Violet gently by the arm was a beaming Stefan, who reached out his other hand toward her.

"Miss Elizabeth!" he said as she took his dear hand. "Thank goodness you're safe."

"The chief says that law enforcement has been watching the place for several days now," Sadie said. "And that county sheriff, Bladen, is as crooked as they come."

Liz settled among them happily, answering their questions, describing her experience at the Hoffman farm, Penny's involvement in Benedikt Hoffman's scheme, as well as the little she knew about Rex Bladen's complicity. "But I never dreamed that the real mastermind of the operation was June Anderson."

Mary Ann came and sat down beside Liz. "And to think we *quilted* with her. She actually stole from her own gallery?"

Jackson nodded. "It wasn't a bad scheme, as schemes go. She could make an insurance claim, and she could also fence the stolen goods. Essentially, she'd get paid twice if she pulled it off."

"Well," Naomi said, "I feel bad for her husband."

"So do I," Liz said. "The chief says Karl was absolutely stunned. Their marriage was in trouble, and he was aware she was drifting away from him, had changed in ways he didn't like. He was about to ask her for a divorce, but she convinced him to take her to the inn for their anniversary."

"Let me guess," Sadie said. "She told him the trip was a last-ditch effort to save their marriage. But what she really wanted was to keep an eye on her operation."

"You guessed right," Liz said. "She's not talking, but Karl's convinced she was planning to take the millions she'd get from selling the stolen artwork and run off somewhere to start a new life without him."

"What about Penny and Benedikt?" Naomi asked.

"They're in custody too. Penny's temporary assignment with the town of Pleasant Creek has ended sooner than anyone expected. The FBI has been called, and they're on their way," Jackson said. "And they all might have gotten away with it if it weren't for Liz." Pride was evident in his voice.

He hadn't strayed far from her, standing protectively behind her chair as her friends gathered around. He was so close, Liz could feel the warmth of him against her back, almost feel his heartbeat. She had to admit to herself that she liked the feeling.

"You should have seen Liz in action," Jackson continued. "She saved herself and Reece from whatever fate those creeps had planned."

Liz looked away, humbled by his praise and by the kindness of her friends. Best of all, Reece was safe and reunited with Lovina. She felt sure that things would be different between them after what Reece had experienced. Maybe Reece would even give up her life in New York and move home to be with her grandmother. Joy welled up inside her. She felt herself smiling, unable to stop.

"How lucky for you—for all of us—that the police chose last night to make their move." Mary Ann took Liz's hand.

Liz shook her head. "It wasn't luck at all. Law enforcement had been watching the farm, yes. But someone called them in last night."

"Who?" Sadie demanded.

"Would you believe it? Mrs. Steele."

"What? That creepy housekeeper? She wasn't in on the whole thing?"

Liz smiled. "She was. But when I was captured and thrown into the room with Reece, Mrs. Steele realized that things might get out of hand. She was willing to go along with the operation for a cut of the proceeds. But she wasn't willing to be a party to murder."

"Well, what do you know?" Sadie said. She pressed herself between the Holmes sisters, hooking an arm through Vera's on the left and Violet's on the right. "Let's talk about something else—something infinitely more pleasant. Vera and I had a long talk, and we have some good news to tell you, Liz," she said, her eyes sparkling. "Don't we, Vera?"

Vera gave a resounding harrumph that lacked her usual acerbity. She brushed a nonexistent thread from her tweed jacket. With a sidelong glance at Stefan, she said with precise enunciation, "Apparently there's going to be a wedding, and it seems to me that the Olde Mansion Inn is just the place to hold the happy event." She jutted her chin forward and peered at Violet's beaming face. "Don't you agree, sister?"

Cheers erupted from all the Material Girls, and Violet clasped her hands together in delight.

When the hubbub died down, Sadie clapped her hands. "All right, girls, enough lollygagging. We have customers to help. Hop to it!"

Opal and Caitlyn went to tend to patrons at the front of the booth while Naomi and Mary Ann wrapped parcels and restocked the tables. Sadie gave Liz and Jackson a penetrating and somewhat sly glance. "We're all set here. You two should go get some coffee. Liz had quite a night last night."

Jackson took Liz by the hand. "Sounds like a good idea," he said, and as he steered her away from the group, he whispered, "Are you sure you're all right?"

"I am," she responded contentedly, leaning her head against his shoulder as they walked. "Thanks to you and friends who care." Lovina's words echoed in her mind: *You hold on to what you love.*

Jackson led her to a sheltered spot behind the line of booths and put his arms around her. They stood together for a long moment, neither wanting to end the embrace. When Liz's phone suddenly rang, they stared at each other in surprise. She looked at the screen and her heart swelled even further than it already was. She connected the call. "Steve!"

"It's me!" came the beloved voice that brought tears to Liz's eyes. "I hope I haven't called at a bad time. What time is it, anyway?"

She laughed. Steve never could keep track of the time difference between Kosovo and Pleasant Creek. Liz looked up at Jackson, glad he was sharing this moment with her. "It's nearly noon," she said into the phone, "but it's never a bad time to hear your voice."

"I couldn't wait to tell you," Steve said. "My tour of duty is done, and I've decided not to reenlist. I'm coming home."

Liz held her breath, then let it out. "Home to Boston?"

He burst out laughing. "No! That's not home anymore. I'm coming where you are—to Pleasant Creek."

Liz felt her heart soar. What could be more perfect? This last week had seen its share of mystery and danger, but here she was safe at home, warmed by the love of friends and the promise that her son was coming home. She couldn't stop the tears that rained down.

"Mom?"

"I'm here," she said, swallowing the flood of emotion. "I can't tell you how happy I am. And I can't wait to welcome you home."